WHO DO YOU LOVE?

WENDELL PRIESTER

outskirtspress

DENVER, COLORADO

Outskirts Press, Inc.
http://www.outskirtspress.com

ISBN: 978-1-4787-1659-4

Outskirts Press and the "OP" logo are trademarks belonging to Outskirts Press, Inc.

Special Thanks to:
My father, Ernest Priester and my mother, Helen Priester,
and my mother –in-law, Nell Butler
brothers and sister-Les Priester, Jonathan Priester, Tal Moore
and also much love and thanks to all my family and friends

A special thanks goes to Alvin Jones for his inspiration and his
friendship. Thanks to the best studio.
And finally, a special thanks goes to my wife, Erica and my two sons,
Ellis and Tommie who
have been the rock in my life and given me unconditional love that
has
sustained me throughout the years. To Pastor Paul Ballard at North
Trenholm Baptist Church in Columbia, S.C. for helping me with
recovery and deliverance

Contents

Ephesians 2: 1-5

1 As for you, you were dead in your transgressions and sins, **2** in which you used to live when you followed the ways of this world and of the ruler of the kingdom of the air, the spirit who is now at work in those who are disobedient. **3** All of us also lived among them at one time, gratifying the cravings of our sinful nature and following its desires and thoughts. Like the rest, we were by nature objects of wrath. **4** But because of his great love for us, God, who is rich in mercy, **5** made us alive with Christ even when we were dead in transgressions--it is by grace you have been saved.

Chapter 1
What is Love?...........
According to Who?

Confrontation thickened the air at the suburban home of Dr. Paul Howard and his wife Cathy. Lauren practiced piano in preparation for a recital, her face serious and a near replica of her mother's. David sat amidst a menagerie of tracks and disconnected tracks, his mouth "choo choo"ing, incessantly. Paul, as usual, was hurrying to his medical practice. Cathy paced the Italian marble in the living room, waiting. Paul rushed in, tossed his briefcase on a black leather Joseph Hoffman chair, and finished straightening his tie.

Cathy, a tall, amber-eyed woman, stood with crossed arms, her lips pressed together, almost disappearing. Her voice sounded hoarse as if she had spent the evening shouting or weeping. "Finally, after waiting up for you to come home late last night, I gave up. I thought this morning we would have a chance to talk about what's going on."

"What's going on?" Paul checked his reflection in the simple black framed mirror.

"What's going on?" She repeated amber eyes suddenly watery. She seemed suddenly hesitant as if the storm that had been brewing had died prematurely. "Why," she asked, softly, "why should I have to beg for your time and affection? It's been so long since I've had any attention from you that I've forgotten how it feels. And the kids—don't you think that the children need a little of your time as well? Lauren and David would love to see their father at a school function or at one of their ball games cheering like a maniac with the rest of the dads!"

Paul turned away from the mirror and rubbed his hand across his dark hair. "Cathy, you don't think that I want to be there? Come on. I miss my family just as much as anyone else, but you know the practice is demanding. *We* have chosen a lifestyle and that lifestyle requires that I go the distance.

"*We* enjoy every minute of it. But *we* want you, too. I didn't think we were trading you for nice furniture and vacations. But let me ask: are we?"

A long sigh hissed through Paul's teeth. "Let's talk tonight. I'm running late and if I don't leave in a minute the traffic will be horrible."

"Fine," Cathy visibly stifled further comment, as Lauren and David entered the room.

"Bye, Daddy!" Lauren called as she slung her shoulder pack and headed for the door. David simply threw up deuces.

"Bye, Daddy loves you."

Paul eased his Porsche Turbo out of the driveway as the children climbed into the neighbor's SUV, heading for school. He loved this car. It had played a major role in motivating him toward success. Unfortunately, nothing killed the success buzz like tension with the wife. He sank into his thoughts only to be retrieved by the melodic tune of his cell phone.

"Hello, Mother." Louise's voice was edgy. "Paul, Cathy just called me. What's going on?"

Second time he'd been asked that question in a day, and it was only 7:45. "Nothing's going on, Mother. I figured Cathy would call you, but I don't have time to discuss this with you because I'm on my way to work."

"Paul, just listen to me. Cathy and the children need more of you. I'm not trying to place the blame on you. I understand where you've been, but does Cathy? I know that we both have been through a lot and your father deserting us and all has not helped. To this day I say God bless the Seawells because I don't know what we would have done if he hadn't come along, but I knew that this would begin to have an effect on you at some point in your life. I still have not come to terms with myself for hanging you over that bridge. Just saying I was in the middle of a psychotic break down doesn't give me permission to forgive myself. Shouldn't motherhood have overridden my depression? I ask myself that every day."

"Mother, I can't go into that right now. I'm okay. I'm still alive. I forgive you, so forgive yourself. Besides Mother this is not the kind of topic I want to face before an extremely full day."

"Okay, Paul. Just think about what I've said. Cathy may need to know these things, if you haven't shared them with her already, to understand things better."

"I'll talk with you later. I love you."

"Bye."

"Bye, Mother."

Chapter 2
The Doctor is In

After parking his car in the hospital parking garage Paul hurried into his office and checked in with his nurse. "Good morning, Nancy."

"Good morning, Dr. Howard."

"How are our patients this morning? How did Phillip do last night?"

Glancing at a clipboard in front of her she said," Well, Doctor Howard, here are the charts from last night for you to review. As of right now, everyone has been served breakfast. In regard to Phillip's condition, he remained stable during the night with no major complications or changes."

"Thanks, Nancy; after I review the charts, I'll start my rounds. I should be back in a couple of hours."

Wearing his white coat, Dr. Howard entered Phillip's room. "Hello, Phillip, how are you doing today?"

"I have seen better days, but all is well. And how is Doctor Howard doing today?"

"Well, I guess that I've seen better days as well. Thanks for asking. I mean thanks really. People seem to think us doctors are beyond the pain and sorrows of everyday life. I have some personal issues that I'm dealing with. Again, thanks for asking."

"Dr. Howard. You can tell me anything. I'm a good listener."

"Two words: The Wife. ." Glancing down at the chart, he said, "Phillip, the tests have shown that you have cirrhosis of the liver."

"Oh. Well that's…news. Of course, I've heard the term, but what does it really mean?"

"Cirrhosis is a disease in which the liver cells become permanently damaged and the damaged areas are replaced by scar tissue through which the blood does not flow properly. In turn, the crucial role that the liver plays in the body disrupts the normal body functions."

"It came from all the drinking, right?"

"Even though alcohol abuse is sometimes directly related to cirrhosis, not all alcoholics develop cirrhosis. Even so, thousands of Americans die each year from the disease. We have found that 75 to 80% of these cases would be non-existent by merely eliminating alcohol abuse. Alcohol-related cirrhosis usually develops after ten or more years of heavy drinking—so to answer your question—yes, it came from the drinking."

"Okay…. So where do we go from here? Are the tests the absolute determinate that I have cirrhosis of the liver?"

"That's what I'm going to discuss with you now. We

wanted to do a liver biopsy to be completely certain that our diagnosis is correct. A liver biopsy is a definite way to diagnose cirrhosis, but with your past history of clotting problems we are not able to perform the procedure. Also, with the symptoms that you are experiencing such as sleep disturbances, ulcers, and vomiting blood, we are 99.9% sure that it is cirrhosis."

Phillip sank deep into the bed. "Bottom line: is this it for me, Dr. Howard?

Paul tried a more cheerful face. "Not if I can help it. What we are going to do is put you on the list for a liver donor. We need to perform the liver transplant as soon as possible, so that you can be around for a while."

"Will the transplant save my life?"

"In my professional opinion, yes, but time is crucial. I am going to have Nancy put you on the list as an emergency. By doing that, we should be able to match you with a donor right away." He gazed at the man in bed but neither spoke until Doctor Howard said, "Any more questions?"

"Not right now. You've given me a lot to think about."

"I want you to know that this is a serious surgery, but we perform many transplants of this nature and our complications have been at a minimal occurrence. Even so, we are still quite cautious... If you come up with any questions in the meantime, feel free to contact me at the office."

Leveling his gaze at the doctor the patient said, "Doc, I have one question for you."

"Well before you ask I have one for you. Phillip," he said, his eyes seeking the man's, "you have such a beautiful family, so why so much drinking?"

"It's funny that you're asking me that. I've been planning to write a book about my life, and that tape on the nightstand is my memoir. It seems now I may need to finish it quicker than I thought. I'll trust that you'll listen to it carefully and then you will know the answers."

"You can entrust me with your tape. I'll be leaving the hospital within the hour to attend a board meeting with the state Parks and Recreation."

"Oh. What are you doing with them?"

"We're discussing a proposal to erect a new monument in the park. I'll listen to it on the way to the meeting. I promise."

Phillip nodded with a benign smile on his face.

Paul hurried back to his office to gather his notes for the meeting. As he turned to remove his jacket from the coat rack, his gaze bounces from his wedding ring then to the prestigious degrees and awards that lined his office walls. His eyes darted from one to another. His mind is whirling and a song from "The Sounds of Music" haunts his memory. "These are a few of my favorite things." Outside in the parking lot he hops in his candy apple red Porsche. Before pulling off, he sits there admiring the craftsmanship of the fine Italian leather seats he had imported from Italy. *Could Cathy be right? Am I really a materialist?* He then starts the engine and begins to listen to the tape.

Chapter 3
The Kid in Me

The tape begins with Phillip speaking as if caught in the middle of conversation.

I begged my mother to let me join the football team. She agreed but my father was against it because the games were scheduled on Sunday. I would always look to the sidelines in hopes of my family being there to encourage and cheer me on, but it was always the other kids' families that did the cheering and encouraging. I wish just once that my dad would have been there when I made a tackle, to hear the announcer call out my name and number. My family would finally arrive after church. I'd watch them walking towards me with their Bibles in hand, shaking their tambourines and acting like they were still in church. I don't know why they bothered getting out of the car. The game was over; everyone has left and only I was left there alone. My mother would always ask me if we won, but everyone knew that the tension was so thick in the car that you could cut it with a knife. It was as if my mother was torn between her husband and her child. But, we all knew that Father's agenda came first and that was supporting his ministry.

Finally, without warning, he took me off of the team. We only had three more games remaining in the season and I couldn't play. Our team ended up undefeated and went on to win the League championship. I couldn't believe that I had to miss the excitement of playing in a championship game! All of my teammates told me that they missed me being there. We had come so far together. Even so, they always treated me as part of the team. So, when they won, I also won.

My coach visited my home the day after the game to ask my father if I could attend the awards banquet. My father told him that I could, but I knew that he would not be there with me... Still, I was excited about going to the banquet.

The night of the banquet came and as usual everyone else's parents and friends and backers were there for support. The banquet room was all festooned with decorations. The team cheerleaders in cute little short skirts, leaped and jumped, twirling their pom poms to everyone's delight. The camaraderie between everybody was great. Everyone was a cheerleader for their player. Only, I was alone.

My team received two trophies - one for an undefeated season and the other for the League championship. When the announcer called the jersey number for the most valuable player of the season, the MVP I was listening, but it did not register that he was calling *my* jersey number until I felt everyone's eyes on me. Then the announcer called my name. "Number forty-eight, Phillip Henry, come up and get your trophy." In the pandemonium, all of my teammates were pulling and pushing me to go up, but I still hesitated because I thought that he had made a mistake. I couldn't believe it. Me?

The parents in the audience were crying and hugging me along with teammates. I was overcome with pride and happiness. My coach shed a few tears as he watched a spontaneous reaction of pure unadulterated joy as the entire team tackled me to the floor.

I will never forget those guys. That moment will stay forever etched in my mind. It was the greatest moment of my life.

My father and I were happy on that day, but for different reasons. He was excited and proud of his new sanctuary and I was excited about my two trophies and being appreciated as "Most Valuable Player." This disconnect between us is what I resented most in my life. Lots of guys didn't have fathers. I had one, but he didn't care about me.

My father's new church building was an ongoing project that I thought would never end. The only cool part of it was that I was able to use sledgehammers to knock down walls while laughing and joking. It was a Freudian kind of thing, this knocking down of walls of my father's church. I guess child labor is okay if you're paid with food instead of money. In my case, McDonalds was the choice of monetary exchange. My incentive to work hard was my "pay increase" from a Happy Meal to a double cheeseburger, large fries, apple pie, and milkshake. His wages were so appealing that he was able to recruit other children in the neighborhood to help on the project.

The church was in a diverse neighborhood. I guess, like anywhere, there were some people I liked and others I'd wish not to see again. As the work on the church began to come to an end then I began getting acquainted with the "boys in the hood." I saw things that I had never seen before and learned things that I never knew anything about. No one was watching over me.

My family seemed to be doing their own thing. Everyone had their own interests, agendas, and desires. By the time I reached eighteen, I began to withdraw from the Church. I was looking for something that at the time I didn't seem to be getting from the Church. So, I was in and out of church. It seemed to me that it was time for me to live my life the way that I wanted.

There were drugs, violence, and crime in the church neighborhood. I met many people who were drawn to me like a magnet because of my outgoing and free spirited nature. I capitalized on opportunity. Everybody knew Phillip. I was hanging out and drinking everyday in one place or another, not to mention "spreading my love around." Even through all of this, I would still go to church but not as often.

I grew up in the Church, so when I did show up I would always be asked to play the drums and sometimes they would ask me to sing. Playing the drums was a gift and passion of mine. Through the rhythm of the drums, I had the gift to reach the souls of many people. In fact, playing music kept me coming back to the Church.

Chapter 4
My First Love

There was one particular occasion that I remember just as if it happened only hours ago. My band was opening for Hootie and the Blowfish at the Coliseum. The day of the concert came with a lot of anticipation, but we knew that we could bring it. The atmosphere was electric with excitement and young people everywhere; a concert was the ultimate experience.

I scanned the crowd on the lookout for a pretty girl.

As we played our final song, Slow Mo in Irmo, I locked eyes with the most beautiful girl in the place. After our set, I quickly ventured out into the audience to find her, but there was no sign of her. I thought that I would die! I had let her slip away from me.

As Hootie and the Blowfish blew the crowd away with "Let Her Cry," I borrowed a pair of binoculars and scanned the crowd again to no avail. With that disappointment, I reverted back to my old habits of drinking and hanging out. I was just wasting my time doing nothing. Then one day, my cousin and I went to check out this new movie, and there she was. My mouth flew open, but nothing came out. Then I heard someone yell out, "Karen." My cousin happened to know this mystery girl and her name was Karen. This time I did not let her get away, I introduced myself right away. My night was now complete. This time I remembered to get her number. I wasn't going to make the same mistake twice. Today, I can hardly remember what I said to her, I was so mesmerized. All I knew for sure is that I came away with her number.

I couldn't wait to get home to call her, but it was too late so I lay in bed staring at the ceiling all night replaying our conversation over and over, savoring her voice, every inflection, every sliver of tone. Without regret, I had fallen instantly in love.

I thought of Karen all day at work, unable to think of anything else. I had asked her to page me at four, and sure enough, she paged me. I had to have some privacy to talk; so I found me a spot in the corner office where it was cozy and quiet. I think that a woman loves to hear the excitement and anticipation in a man's voice that is for her and only her. It tells her how much he is thinking about her. I think that she felt that from me. Before I knew it, we had talked for hours. It was interesting to know that we were alike in a lot of ways in that we both enjoyed talking about the Bible and that we were both PK's (preacher's kids).

Our relationship was moving at a rapid pace, because before I knew it I had met her parents and then it became "official" –we were a couple. The connection between us was almost surreal in that we were so mesmerized by each other. With little thought, I

jumped into this relationship head first while putting my exposed heart directly into her hands.

My whole life revolved around Karen. With her, my life was a blank sheet of paper. As our relationship flourished, we began to write the chapters.

It felt as if life was climbing to a climax, to a happily-ever-after. Karen and I started to again go to church and in turn became more committed. I also got involved with the Youth on the Move program by participating in various projects in the church and throughout the community. I stopped hanging out with my old buddies from the neighborhood, instead; I started hanging out with people who believed in taking a positive stand in what they believed. Not to mention, the relationship between our families was drawn even closer. I could only thank Karen for this.

Then our first major obstacle surfaced. During Karen's senior year of high school she had to decide whether she would attend Clemson University or Oral Roberts University. Karen's parents wanted her to attend Oral Robert's University because of its Christian culture, but I wanted Karen to attend Clemson because it was where she wanted to go and for my own selfish reasons—it was closer. But, that decision was still months away, so in the meantime, Karen and I just continued writing our romance. The closer that Karen and I got the less time we talked about the Bible and the more we concentrated on each other. We were aware of our feelings and we were anxious to take our relationship to the "next level."

When it happened between us it was, of course, magical. With us, what else could it be? I will never forget that day. I picked her up from school and took her home with me. I knew that we would have hours alone before my parents arrived. While I was in the kitchen preparing us a snack, I could hear her calling me. From the tone in her voice, I could tell that she was ready to make this happen and I was ready to oblige. In a daze and before I knew it, I had removed her clothes and we made love for the first time on the white carpet of my parents' living room. It was great in so many ways but mostly because it created a bond between us, but in the same respect, I felt like we had tasted of the forbidden fruit. It was like ice cream topped with guilt.

From that point on, our relationship rose to a new level. It was at that point that Karen's parents, sensing our new commitment, strongly suggested that we stop seeing each other. It was as if they saw the road that their daughter was traveling and they wanted to create a detour before anything destructive happened--like her getting pregnant.

Karen and I tried to adhere to her parents' demands, but the bond between us was too deep, or so I thought.

As she approached the last few months of high school, Karen let me know that she had decided to go to Clemson. That was good news. With everything spiraling out of control, I was happy again because I thought that would be the bridge back to Karen. I needed her so badly because I had returned to hanging out with my old buddies again.

I knew that if we could be together then everything would be all right. My instincts had always been good; they just needed a bit of guidance.

But with Karen's transition to college, I noticed a change in her behavior towards me. She started to distance herself from me and was hanging out more and more with her college friends. I was feeling left out and left behind. I knew what was coming next, but I wanted to see how long she would try to go through the motions. Finally Karen owned up to what I already knew. It was over between us.

Karen truly believed that this was best for both of us, but she just didn't know how deeply this let me down, which meant of course, that I had loved her more than she loved me. Karen had been my first love and I was deeply hurt. I felt the pain to the depths of my soul. I was depressed and moped around listening to sad love songs and feeling them personally, very personally. Not only was my heart broken, but I felt rejected by both Karen and the Church, two things that I held close to my heart. With the feeling that the Church didn't want me because they secretly ousted me out of the Youth Group (presumably, because they had heard of my past unrestrained partying) and Karen not wanting to be with me, I went back to alcohol and my old buddies. I knew that I could always count on them no matter what.

I have made many mistakes in my life just as most of us have, but I would not give up. I felt as though my soul was dead and that my body was a corpse among the living dead and that I was simply going through the motions of life. I was, in effect, an emotional zombie. I didn't have a relationship with anyone—not even God. I couldn't remember the last time I had prayed. I was doing things that I thought I would never do, saying things that I would never say. I felt like nothing else mattered to me. I felt cut off and alone. There was nothing spiritual or meaningful in my life. My loneliness was canyon deep.

A year passed with virtually no contact with my family. Then one day I went into the corner store to buy alcohol. As I made my way toward the back of the store to the beer cooler, there was Uncle James. I quickly turned my head in hopes that he wouldn't notice me, but my uncle was very intuitive, especially when it came to me. His look was deep and I'm sure he penetrated to my very soul. As he came over to hug me, I dropped the six-pack of beer. At that moment, I felt the walls that I built around me start to crumble. Uncle James didn't say much. He just told me that he loved me. Those few words gave me the reassurance that I needed to try to pick up the pieces of my life. At that moment, I stood frozen as my life began to flash before my eyes. He was making sense to me, but I had to get out of there because I didn't want him to see me break down. Before we said our good-byes, he urged me to contact my mother because both he and I knew that it was her prayers that have kept me alive. He said that it would be a joy to her to know that I was okay.

I promised to get in touch with my mother. We then said our good-byes and I left and drove to the park. As I sat in the car alone, I looked at myself in the rearview mirror and I thought about my life and what I'd become. I thought back on this year I'd lost living day-to-day accomplishing nothing while drinking. On impulse, I made the decision to seek help again by attending Alcoholics Anonymous.

Even though I attended two recovery meetings a week, I still drank every day. I just wasn't up to kicking booze, cold turkey, at least not yet. I did contact my mother more frequently now for moral support, but I knew that she had become frustrated with me because I was still drinking. In her voice, I would easily detect swirls of sadness and joy and regret. Her ambivalence was understandable. I knew that she was happy because I had sought out help, but she was very sad because her baby boy was an alcoholic. Not to mention, my drinking reminded her of the old wounds and scars of her past. My mother's family had a history of drinking problems, and it saddened her deeply to see me ride down the same collision course. I told her that it was hard for me to quit drinking. I knew I had a real monkey on my back but I also knew I would never give up the fight.

With the struggle always before me, I continued with the recovery process. I began to see some progress. Before long, I admitted to my problem of alcohol and that my life had become unmanageable. I came to believe that only a power greater than I could restore me to sanity. I took a searching fearless moral inventory of myself and humbly asked God to remove my shortcomings and to give me strength. Through prayer and meditation, I sought out how to improve myself and how to carry out these steps effectively. As a result, I began drinking less and started to feel good about myself, but unfortunately, though, the empty void in my life seem to expand even greater. I had heard about the black, holes in space. They say they are endless. That's how I saw my own.

So in order to fill it, I poured in more alcohol in hopes to bury or at least mask the pain. Eventually, I fell back into the same rut and became more social with less treatment, but in the back of my mind I was still determined not to give up the struggle.

Chapter 5
My Savior

One day, my friends and I decided to hang out after work at this hot new spot. They knew that I had been down on myself and that I could use a good time. They knew that I would be ready for whatever sounded like fun, so we decided to get ready for the night by getting toasted the minute the clock struck 5 p.m. By the time, we arrived at the club that night we had accomplished just that; we were feeling just right. We were what we called, "prepared."

That night, the club was packed to capacity. I was like a kid in the candy store with a pocketful of quarters. The music, drinks, and women were right and I knew that something good was going to happen that night.

The alcohol had me hyped, so I began prowling to find me a honey. As the night went on, dance after dance, drink after drink, I scanned the room to see what was out there. First, I saw this tall statuesque goddess, standing in the corner so I asked her to dance. Before she answered, she gave me a once over look. Her attitude screamed that she was stuck on herself, but it didn't matter to me because I thrived on the challenge. We made our way to the dance floor, but her dance moves were a bit stuffy and stiff. She raised her brows at my inhibited style. As I made a spin move, her friend cut in to dance with me. Now, her friend was much prettier than her and she knew how to dance. She rolled her hips and dropped it just the way I like it. She smiled at me like she knew what I was thinking. I was hypnotized. The music stopped, but I was still there. There was something about her that I couldn't let go. Through that one dance, I could detect the innocence and honesty in her character. I introduced myself to her and Sharon—that was her name, my beautiful rose of Sharon-- gave me that all knowing smile again. She then turned away from me as if she was looking for someone; almost as if she was lost. I started to think that she shooting me down. But I didn't give in that easily, I asked for her number. She said that she would give me her number as soon as she found her friends, so she took my hand and we went off to find them in the crowd. As soon as we found them, true to her word, she gave me her contact numbers.

At the end of the night, I didn't take her home; I didn't sleep with her; and I didn't drink any more that night. But I didn't care. I had found something important. There was something special about her. There was a difference in her, something that I didn't see in any of the other girls who I had met. She had this sense of innocence about her that made me feel at home with her. And I might say, rather protective. It was as if she knew everything about me, but accepted me for who I was. Once again, I fell in love, but this time it was different, because I felt that I had met my savior.

The next day, I called Sharon and there were the sounds of laughing women in the background. I could imagine that they were discussing last night's events. In desperate hopes that our meeting last night was as good as it felt, I was anticipating hearing the tone in her voice. When she reached the phone, she sounded excited and giddy. I was relieved to know that the feeling was mutual between us.

Our initial conversation was cordial, but still intimate. We both were curious about each other's background from where we were born to where we worked. Never slow when it came to the ladies, I immediately asked her when I could see her again. She agreed to meet that evening. My mind was flooded with thoughts of her all day. I couldn't wait to get the evening started. After work, I rushed home to shower and dress. I called her to get directions to her apartment.

As I entered The Park Apartment Complex, I must say that I was impressed. No low rent here; it was all about luxury. I was relieved I had not come empty-handed. At the door, I presented her with a chilled bottle of Reisling.

The conversation was so pleasant, so peaceful it was almost surreal. I found myself wondering why she was not already taken. With as much tact as possible, I asked her if she was in a relationship and she told me that she had been out of a relationship for about six months.

She went on to describe her ex- as jealous and possessive. Even though they were not dating any longer, he still tracked her whereabouts. So, it was not unheard of for him to pop up at her apartment unannounced. I told her that if he decided to pop in tonight that I could handle it. Little did Sharon know that I had some street in me, and one of the main rules of the street was never to be caught unprepared?

She relaxed again and we enjoyed the evening. It was getting late and I didn't want to overstay my welcome, so we shared a hug and said goodbye.

The next day, Sharon called me to see if I wanted to hang out after work. We decided to meet at a French bistro in the Vista for dinner and drinks.

We were so engrossed in our conversation that we lost track of time. We had a good bit to drink, so I asked Sharon if it would be okay for me to crash at her apartment. At first she was hesitant, but she finally agreed on one condition; that I would have to sleep on the couch. I agreed and reassured her that I would be a perfect gentleman.

When we arrived at her apartment, to my surprise, Sharon asked me a pointed question. She asked about my drinking. I kind of played it down by claiming that I had built up a massive tolerance for it. I did not allude to her that it was one of my major problems because I didn't want her to think that this would be a problem in our relationship. And it wasn't something I was particularly proud of. I think that she was okay with my answer because she never made mention of it again. But from being around

Sharon, I could tell that it was still a concern. After that, we focused on the television until we fell asleep.

As time went on, Sharon and I spent every day together. I knew that I was stealing all of her time away from her friends, just as she was taking me away from mine. It was like we both went on an extended romantic getaway. My friends began to question my whereabouts, but I was not going to expose Sharon to that side of me. In the back of my mind, I knew that she had to wonder why she never met any of my buddies because I had met almost all of her friends. For the most part, I knew that her friends were fond of me, and they made it clear they were impressed with my good looks. Still, it was apparent that they still had reservations. Sharon's friends were protective of her because they knew that she could be trusting, but little did they know that I wanted to protect her as well.

Our relationship was becoming serious so Sharon asked me how I felt about the idea of us becoming roommates. Sharon was a good girl so she didn't feel comfortable with the term "living together". Whatever works? I was thrilled with the idea. Eventually, we settled into the routine of a couple's life.

When Sharon and I got tired of playing house and wanted to make it official I knew I would have to meet the parents. Sharon had shared some of her childhood and I knew that her parents were strict disciplinarians. That was evident in the way that Sharon carried herself.

The day we went to meet them was a beautiful, crisp fall morning. Even though the drive was just under an hour, it felt like eternity because of its purpose. I assured my sweetheart over that, having been raised by the good reverend; I was more than able to function in polite company.

As we drove up the steep paved driveway of her parents' home, I could noticed the tell-tale signs of muted wealth, the exquisite landscaping hovering above the almost silent street. It was as if everything was in its rightful place. Before we could ring the doorbell, the door opened and there stood two elderly people. Their maturity caught me off guard; I looked over at Sharon with a puzzled look, and then went on with the introductions and pleasantries. After the introductions, it was clear to me that these were Sharon's grandparents. Apparently they raised her as a child.

As we sat in the great room, I saw them observing my every move and the tension was palpable. Being scrutinized is rough. Even more jarring was how throughout the conversation, they dropped hints about their expectations for Sharon. The expectations were not out of the ordinary. They were the same as of any other parent, but they seemed relentless in delivering them. Sharon became a little agitated with their forwardness and candid questioning. All in all, though, we had an enlightening conversation and I felt as though they approved of me. Before we left they gave me a grand tour of the house, which seemed filled with antiques and untouchable furniture. During the tour, Sharon's grandfather said that hopefully one day Sharon and I could live like this as well. I just gave him a respectful smile and a nod.

On our way home Sharon told me that her grandparents were impressed with me. She asked me what I thought of them and I told her that I thought they were good people, despite being quite opinionated. Even so, I agreed to the arrangement that was set forth by them because at that time I thought that I could be that person. If my friends had known that I had made such an agreement they would laugh because they didn't know that side of me.

The following week we decided to meet my parents. I wanted to give her the full treatment so we decided to meet on the following Sunday. The day started with us attending my father's church where Sharon met my family and church members. While my father was preaching, I saw Sharon looking around the room. As she was doing so, our eyes met and she gave me an amused smile like she wanted to laugh. I guess it was totally different from what she expected. I gave her a quick smile back, because I understood, but I was not ashamed. This was a down-home church. After the service, we ate a feast of a dinner with my family. My mother had prepared a fried turkey, dressing, yams, corn on the cob, macaroni and cheese, turnips, cornbread, and the sweetest of ice tea.

As expected, everyone instantly fell in love with my rose of Sharon. They all complimented her by saying that she was a sweet girl and she is what I needed in my life. Then they began to criticize me and make suggestions about what I should and should not do with my life right in front of Sharon. My family was not nearly as discreet as hers had been. For Sharon's sake, I maintained my composure. After my family's debriefing, Sharon whispered to me that it would take more than that to run her off. We both laughed. I laughed from relief. She actually appeared to be enjoying this crazy bunch.

As more months melted away, we hit something of an impasse. We knew what to expect from each other. We respected and trusted one another. There was no doubt in my mind that she would be the same in years to come. There were times that she gave me subtle hints about marriage. I had entertained the same thoughts. I wanted to get the perspective of an experienced man who had been married for quite some time, especially on topics like sex and romance after tying the knot. Sharon and I talked about responsibility, family structure, and doing what was right like having love and commitment, but never about physical passion. We also didn't talk about our individual goals, dreams or ambitions in life. Naturally, I had some concerns.

I had the opportunity to talk to a guy who had been married for twenty-five years. He told me that many people tend to misunderstand compatibility and miss out on the importance of having a good relationship by primarily seeking passion, romance, and sex. He went on to say that those things will eventually come and grow in your relationship as you get to know and experience one another.

I agreed with what he said because it made sense and seemed logical. Besides, his wife seemed to be happy. I had the perfect girl so maybe now was the time to propose to her. I wanted to be sure so I wrestled with the idea for a while longer, but I guess that I was taking too long because every time that I would speak with my mother she would act like a cheerleader constantly chanting, "It's time." Not to mention, Sharon's parents and friends giving me the third degree asking me what was I waiting for. The pressure was on.

Sharon's parents' plan, which I had tentatively agreed to at our first meeting, went like this. When we married, we would move to their hometown where the apartments were more inexpensive so that we could save money. I would work in the plant. I figured that I have nothing else going on in my life right now so why not. So one night I invited Sharon to dinner. I had been drinking pretty heavy that night.

After dinner, I fell to my knees, stumbling, trying to balance myself. I took her hand and kissed it, and then I looked into her eyes and asked her to marry me. She asked me if I was serious as she blushed with embarrassment because we were in the middle of the restaurant with all eyes on us. Almost as if to avoid a scene, she quickly said yes. We left the restaurant arm in arm and beaming at each other.

Knowing I had been in an alcoholic fog, the next morning Sharon told me what happened at the restaurant and I didn't believe her. She began to laugh as she showed me the engagement ring. She called all of her friends and everybody who knew us to tell them the good news. I grabbed her close to me and looked her in the eyes and asked her if she was sure that she wanted to marry me because I didn't have wealth and I did quite enjoy drinking. Kissing me hard on the lips, she assured me that everything would be fine. We actually thought that we had all the bases covered for a long, fulfilling marriage. The date was set, and the women of the families immediately began making arrangements and planning for the big day while the guys and I were trying to do all the devilment we could before I jumped the broom.

———⫸《()》⫷———

The day of the wedding, I was not nervous just anxious, because this was our special day and I wanted it to go well, but most of all I wanted to get it over. I was the first person at the church, so I walked in and sat down on the front pew to collect my thoughts. A million things were swirling in my head from the past and present. We had no idea as to what the future would bring or where we were headed. All I knew was that a lot was riding on my shoulders. All eyes would be on me to see if I had turned my life around to make a better life with Sharon. Most of them had doubts but it didn't matter to me because I was sure of myself. I still felt like something was missing. I didn't have a college degree, a good job or career. I didn't even have a savings account. The only thing I had to offer Sharon was my love and support. I wished for a father I could talk to right then and there. It didn't have to be all the right answers just some words of encouragement, man to man, father to son, friend to friend. As I considered my options, the moment passed.

The guests began entering the church. Sometimes you just have to go it alone. I just wish it wasn't so often.

The wedding ceremony was unforgettable, beautiful with scripture, song, poetry, and a commitment before God. I viewed Sharon in a different light after that day. Now I was a husband with a wife.

Everything went as planned. We moved to Sharon's hometown into a very nice apartment about five minutes from my job. After about three months of marriage, Sharon and I had settled into our comfort zone. We would race home, jump in the shower, watch Melrose Place and I would drink a twelve pack of beer. After the show I wanted to spend quality time, so I would encourage her to wear my favorite dress and dance for me. That would only be the beginning and then the rest would lead to the bedroom where I would give her a soothing body massage. What else could a man ask for? We were newlyweds. I would often look back to the days we first met and how happy we were. No one marries to fail.

Sharon and I enjoyed having our own privacy in our own space with no interruptions and intrusions until there was an unexpected knock at the door. Sharon and I exchanged a puzzled glance as neither of us was expecting anyone. Sharon rushed to the peephole in the door while yelling, "Just a minute!" She turned to me with terror in her eyes and said that it was her mom and dad. She then began to scurry through the house removing everything from sight she thought that they would disapprove of. I slowly got up from the sofa... damn, this could not be happening. I even hid my beer in my own house out of respect for Sharon. As I made my way back to the bedroom to put on a shirt and pants, I heard them telling Sharon that they were in the neighborhood and wanted to see how we were doing. I didn't buy that story because they knew no one in our apartment complex.

A couple of days later we joked about the incident, and then to my dismay it happened again. I was furious. This time, I stormed to the back room belching out every obscenity that I could think of hoping they would hear me, and they did. I heard them tell Sharon that if it's going to be a problem with them stopping by, then they would not come back. Angry, I mumbled, please, make my day. The only reason we we're here, her mother said, is to deliver a gift. We bought you a washer and dryer.

I had to apologize for overreacting, but I also had to stress to her that I value our quality time alone. If her parents wanted to come over, they should show us the common courtesy of calling first. Sharon agreed and called them up the next day. Her grandfather didn't take to the request too well. He solemnly vowed not to step foot in our home again. Of course, he didn't mean it because within the month they were back at it. Her parents were persistent and sometimes annoying, but they made sure we had everything we needed. I didn't want to sever those ties.

Along with dealing with her parents coming over unannounced, I had to deal with the fact that our sex life was almost non-existent. Before we were married, I never pushed the issue about our sex life and giving each other affection because I respected her morals. But now she was my wife, and I wanted to share that intimacy with her. Every day we would do our same routine after work shower, drink, *Melrose Place*, etc. When it came to the part where I led her to the bedroom and began the touching and rubbing, she began to show resistance. Even cuddling didn't soften her up.

My cravings for affection grew. I wanted to hold her close to me and kiss her on the lips and tell her how much I loved her, but she pushed me away. Eventually, I stopped trying. I needed to know what was wrong. When I asked her if there was a problem she said nothing. That night I lay in the dark staring at the ceiling trying to decipher what I was doing wrong and what to do about it. This went on well into the morning hours.

The next day as we were preparing for work there was tension in the air. As we left the house, we were cordial with our good-byes. All day at work I couldn't concentrate for thinking about the issue. Maybe she needed a change of pace, so I called her up like when we first met and invited her to dinner. I was thrilled that she accepted my invitation. We apologized to each other about the previous night, but she never spoke of what caused her actions. Maybe, just maybe this was what we needed to get back on track.

We went to our favorite bistro in the Vista and drank our favorite wine while being serenaded by the mellow tones of a string quintet. The night was perfect. It was going so well I thought that this would be the perfect time to show her how much I love to have her next to me, so we left the bistro in a hurry like newlyweds all over again. We made out as soon as we got home and then there was silence as we lay next to each other. Sharon fell asleep as I remained awake wondering if something was wrong with me. While making out, I didn't feel the passion I thought I'd feel between two people who say they love each other. It was like she was waiting for me to finish my business. So the next day I felt I had to talk to her about the way I was feeling.

After going through our same routine after work, I expressed to her how much I wanted to bring some excitement into the bedroom, talk about sex, oral sex, and sexy talk. She paused and looked into my eyes as if she was struggling with that issue. After a long moment of silence she informed me that my ideas were farfetched, nasty and unheard of... Girls who perform those acts do not make good wives. She felt that she would be compromising her morals and values. We went in circles on this issue and she stood firm. So I ended the conversation even though I disagreed. I was not happy with her way of thinking but I had to live with it.

One day after work, I went to hang out with a co-worker to have a few drinks. I thought it was a good idea for me to get out of the normal routine at home. I called Sharon to let her know that I would be hanging out with a buddy, but I don't think that she was thrilled about it.

Before we ate, we drank a bottle of Crown Royal and talked about our situations. I thought I, finally I had a friend that I could talk to that understood. We had a good time and the drinks were rolling. I was feeling right. We drove to my house where we took the last sip of Crown and vowed that we must do it again. I went inside wanting to talk to Sharon, but she, dressed in flannels, pulled hard away from me. Despite, the flannels, my physical hunger for her arose. Loud, probably slurring, I made the mistake of asking for sex, only I said something like coochy. That was the wrong move. It sparked our first argument and it was not pleasant. I told her how I felt about her not wanting me to touch her and having no emotion during our most intimate moments. I never had that problem in the past. And she talked about my drinking too much. Raging, I said, "Let's get everything out in the open, maybe you would be happier"…and I stopped. The room fell quiet. I had passed out.

I woke up the next morning apologizing, but she was hardly accepting of my attempt to make amends. I traveled to Columbia frequently visiting strip clubs and hanging with the guys then coming home drunk.

My wife and I were obviously growing apart. Her family noticed things were not going well because I would skip church and they would call Sharon inquiring my whereabouts and she didn't know what to say. I would do the right thing for a couple of days, but then I'd go back to my unwholesome ways.

One particular night I attended a Mike Tyson and

Holyfield fight party in Columbia with a couple of my friends and we partied until the wee hours of the morning. I was loaded and on the prowl. I bumped into an old flame, and she showed me what I was missing at home. Filled with guilt, I tried driving home, the last bottle of Paul Mason at my side. . As I bobbed and weaved across the highway, still sipping from the bottle but terrified, begging God to please let me make it home safe. Two blocks from my house I was stopped, arrested and taken to jail. I woke up behind bars not knowing what happened and why I was there. I called Sharon, which I hated to do, because I knew that she would be hysterical. She told me that she had friends searching the highways and calling the hospitals looking to see if I had an accident. I felt awful. When I got home I called everybody to let them know that I was all right. I cried as I took a long hot shower because I knew that this was a huge setback for me, and I knew I couldn't stop myself from drinking. This incident pushed me and Sharon even further apart, but I still saw her as my savior. I felt as though I let her down. She was still crying as I got out of the shower. Her eyes were still swollen from her sleepless night. And then she let me hear exactly what was on her mind. She let me have it. She told me that I was just like her biological mother in that I would always apologize, but I never followed up the words with action. She went on to say how she was always the one to pick up the broken pieces.

This was the first time that I ever heard Sharon speak of her mother during our whole relationship. I was beginning to understand why she behaved the way she did. She had built a wall of defense because she had been let down as a child.

She ended by saying that her parents could not find out about this. My mind was filled with confusion, disappointment, sadness, and pain.

I knew I had to make a change and fast. It would be a day to day process and I would have to be diligent and persistent to see it through.

My first step was to get involved with positive activities so I returned to the Church.

When I was at church, I felt a sense of belonging because I was able to return to the passion of playing the drums and singing. If someone didn't know me they would think that I was two different people because the DUI Phillip and Church Phillip were like night and day. It has been several months now and I have been sober for two of them. Sharon constantly reminded me of her being proud of me. I would always remind her that it will take one day at a time.

Sharon came to me one night as we were relaxing on the couch. She was smiling as if she had just swallowed a canary. She said softly, "Baby, I have been thinking, since you have been doing so well and you are on the right track, I think that it is time that we had a child."

I looked at her and said that I had been thinking about the same thing. I was so happy to hear those words. It gave me confirmation that she thought I was ready to take on the responsibilities of raising a child and taking care of home. I also felt I was ready. I wanted to begin working on it right away but she wanted to tell her parents the good news first.

We were invited to Sharon's parents' house for Sunday dinner. She thought that this would be the perfect time to let them know of our plans to have a baby. While at the dinner table Sharon broke the news. Her father gave us the third degree about our plans of taking care of his grandchild. He went from my temp status at work to attacking our apartment. The bottom line was that he didn't want us to raise his grandchild in an apartment. He suggested that we stay with them to save money towards the down payment of a house.

I thought the nerve of these people! Where do they get off! Nevertheless, I agreed again to their "master plan."

Ultimately, I thought this child would be perfect for our marriage in that it would bring us closer together as a couple and family. We moved into Sharon's parents' as planned and began saving while our house was being built. I couldn't wait until its completion because we forfeited our privacy. I would stay in our bedroom the majority of the time. I would get off work have a beer and go to sleep until the next day. Throughout Sharon's pregnancy I had selfish concerns about adding to our family because when the baby was born there would be less and less time for me. Still, I enjoyed watching the baby as it grew inside her. I'd touch her stomach everyday to let him know that I would always be there. I wondered if my father did the same to my mother before my birth to let me know that he would always be there. I didn't want to fail my child as my father had failed me.

John was God's gift to Sharon and me, and we welcomed him into our new home. I felt it symbolized a new beginning and a fresh start for all of us. We made a vow to give John all the love and affection that he needed to help him grow into a well rounded responsible young man, which may sound a bit hypocritical of me because I had my struggles with responsibility, love, and alcohol.

When John was born my wife did not hold him in her arms to welcome him to the new world. At first I didn't think much of it; I made the assumption that she was exhausted after giving birth. The doctors asked her if she wanted to hold him, she said, "No, I'm afraid I might hurt him." Several weeks passed and she still hadn't held him in her arms, not even so much as to kiss him on the forehead. I would pick him up hold him close to my chest and look into his big brown eyes and tell him that his Daddy loved him and he would smile back at me as if he knew what I was saying. I told him no matter how old he gets or how bad times may become he could count on me. I saw myself in his eyes and the way I wanted to be loved and I couldn't disappoint him.

A year had past and it was John's first birthday. I was excited for him because I wanted him to see and feel the love that we had for him. Both families gathered at our home with toys and gifts that rival Toys R Us. I enjoyed seeing the smile on his face as he blew out the candle and we sang happy birthday. It seemed as if time was passing by so quickly.

I remember one day I had just picked John up from Sharon's parents home and two friends of mine stopped by to visit. Normally I didn't like anyone visiting unannounced because my family space is something that I hold sacred for my family and I to have peace, but I didn't mind about them stopping over because they didn't intend to stay long. I offered them a cold beer just to shoot the breeze and chat a little. The moment we began to take a drink Sharon's father stepped through the door and saw John standing in front of us looking in curiosity. My neighbor who knew him immediately shoved his open beer into his jacket spilling it all over the floor. He began to apologize to my father in law as he tried to grab everything to wipe it clean. Sharon's father didn't seem to be upset with him, but he let me know that John should not be in the presence of my friends and me when we were drinking. I knew he was angry because I saw his lips move in a rapid sequence as he drove away. My friend joked about how he tried to hide his beer in his coat and instead spilled it all over the floor.

The phone rang and it was Sharon. I'm sure that her father had told her what happened because her voice sound agitated. She didn't find humor in the beer spilling. I tried to explain to her that John was playing with his toys and he wandered into the room where we were drinking. She wasn't buying it. I didn't want to make matters worse so I ended the conversation by agreeing with her. We were drifting further apart.

As Sharon and I grew apart, I spent more time with

John. I would watch him play in the backyard with his toys as I cooked on the grill. I wanted Sharon to be there with us, but John and I did everything alone just the two of us. Our bond was getting stronger and stronger each day while there was something missing between Sharon and me. My wife and I knew that we loved each other, but I was no longer in love with her. I was longing for that connection but I was not finding it in her. Maybe it was the environment. She knew I didn't want to live in this little town working a temporary job. It was frustrating. I think that we all were going through the motions.

Unexpectedly, I received a phone call at work requesting that I come home right away. I was apprehensive because for some strange reason I knew something was wrong because the ring tone of the phone gave me a somber feeling. I felt it go through my muscles down to the marrow of my bones. Immediately, I thought the worst. I thought that something terrible had happened to John or Sharon. Immediately, I began praying to God pleading not to let anything crazy have happened to them. I drove the highway like the last lap of the Indy 500. My heart was pounding, my palms were sweating. All I was thinking was that I was going to be alone for the rest of my life. I arrived at the house to see Sharon and her parents holding onto John. I was relieved to see that he was OK. Sharon seemed to be doing well. If they are OK, then what's the emergency? I asked them what was wrong. Sharon raised her head slowly and spoke softly and said that they had to rush my father to the hospital and I needed to get there as soon as possible. My mind was numb. I knew that it could get ugly real fast. As Sharon and I drove to the hospital, I stared in one direction with my eyes straight forward like I was a soldier in boot camp.

Focused and expressionless, I didn't know what to think. Sharon parked the car and looked in my direction and asked was I feeling all right. I broke my trance and said yes. We walked briskly to the hospital entrance. In the distance I saw my mother. Our eyes met and I saw the tears streaming down her face. She dashed towards me with her arms outstretched. She cried out, "He is gone, Phillip, your father has passed away!"

At that moment I didn't feel anything. I didn't know what to say or do. My emotions were null and void. I asked myself should I cry. Should I feel anything? I was at a loss for words but for some strange reason I felt that I needed to see him and touch him to make sure that I was not dreaming. All of those years from the past when I was fatherless it seemed began to flash before my eyes. All of those years when I wanted a relationship with him re-played in my head, now they are gone forever. I told my mother that I needed to see him.

The child part of me was angry with him and didn't want to see him but the adult in me was telling me that it was the right thing to do to show respect. It seemed like an eternity before I arrived at my father's room. As I walked to his room, I was thinking of my "final words" to him. Time was lost. I had so many unanswered questions that I needed to ask him and only he could answer them.

Unfortunately, now they would never be answered.

Finally, I arrived at room number 215 where my father lay motionless on the bed. It was just minutes after his death, so his face was still uncovered and I was able to stand before him face to face. Then like a child, I began asking him a series of questions. "Where did you go, Daddy, when I needed you the most as a child? What happened to keep you away from me? Why didn't you love me? I wanted you to be my buddy, Daddy.

"You were larger than life to me. I always looked up to you. All I wanted was a friend in you. I still see the strength and proudness in your face. What are you taking with you that kept your heart sealed from me all your life? Maybe I could have helped you daddy. We could have had a great relationship."

I slowly lifted his hand and placed it in mine. I knew alive he would never allow me to do this. That was too much affection. Some time had lapsed and his hands were becoming as cold as the room. I continued, "Daddy, I know that you are not a bad person. It is that you didn't know how to express your love to a son?"

After I said my piece, I leaned forward and gave him a kiss on the forehead. Then the strangest event took place as I began to walk out of the room, I reached to open the door and it slowly opened unassisted and a rush of air pushed past my face. I smelled an intense fragrance of peppermint, my father's favorite candy. I was startled as I then turned to face him one last time and departed.

Dealing with my father's death affected me more than

I was willing to admit. Those unanswered questions still haunt me to this day. My sanity was exhausted and I needed a vacation from the temp jobs, seeing Sharon's parents every day and Sharon and I not connecting. Not to mention, my drinking, which was on the rise again? On top of that, I had to prepare myself to make funeral arrangements for my father. I couldn't let my mother torture herself even more. I felt that she needed me now more than ever, so I met with her to discuss the details.

After talking with her for a moment, Mama looked deep into my eyes and asked me if I was still drinking, but I didn't want to let her know that it was spiraling out of control so I answered her by talking around the issue.

She then asked me about taking over my father's church. She went into a spiel about how everybody was wondering about it. Besides, she said that she and Father talked about me being his successor if anything should ever happen to him. Little did she know that I couldn't begin to fill those shoes. Before I knew it, I had answered her abruptly by saying that I wasn't a minister and that my life was not in any order to accept a responsibility such as this. I ended the conversation on that note and diverted her attention back to the matter at hand.

I knew that I had to step up to the plate and take care of Mama. I was traveling from one place to the next making sure that everything went smooth. But my mother did not have to worry about her finances because my father made sure she had enough income so that she wouldn't have to go back to work or depend on anyone. My father always made sure that his family was well taken care of. That was one of the things I admired about him.

The funeral was scheduled for Saturday afternoon at 3 p.m. at my father's church. I knew when I returned there at this time everyone would assume that I would be the next pastor of this church and I don't want them to get that idea. I just wanted to bury my father and get out of there. I didn't want them approaching me asking such questions but sure enough it happened. I had to let them know that I was not ready and God was not ready for me to fill my father's shoes. The ceremony was a peaceful one and I was glad that he was resting.

I saw many of my old friends from the past at the funeral. One in particular was my childhood best friend, Pete.

Chapter 6
All About the Business

Pete related to me that he had become Regional Manager of a growing package delivery company where he had been working for many years. He told me that he had aspirations of becoming its owner and wanted to know if I wanted to be a part of it. This sounded like an opportunity that I couldn't refuse, so I readily said yes. He wanted me to keep in touch with him because he was aligning his contacts and structuring contracts for the takeover and that it was only a matter of time. The business was located in the Columbia, South Carolina area. When I talked it over with Sharon, she agreed to the move because she too was missing all that Columbia had to offer.

With that decision, we decided to take a vacation to Hilton Head to clear our minds and discuss our plans for the move. While we were there Sharon was acting a little different than usual. It was like she had something on her mind that she wanted to tell me. She was being giddy, frisky and a little playful, which was refreshing but out of character for her. This was the time we both needed to get away from the hustle and bustle of everyday life because I knew that when we returned home we would be faced with opposition from her parents because of the move to Columbia. Sure enough, they opposed our decision, but it was our call on the matter and they were not going to overturn it. They accused me of dividing the family. I didn't care about their accusations because I knew that my intentions were that I wanted a better life for my family. On the last night before returning home from Hilton Head I found out why Sharon was so giddy and frisky. She told me that she was pregnant. I was so excited because we needed some good news. I celebrated by toasting the news with a bottle of champagne and Sharon with sparkling grape juice. Again, I over indulged myself and drank until I passed out. I regretted that this happened because I wanted to make a new start and leave all the drinking behind and get my life and my family back to normal.

I spoke with Pete again and he said that in a week's time everything would be finalized and I could begin working with the company. Pete and I met at the company early one morning where we discussed future plans to become owners. He stressed that it could be short-term or a long-term deal, but it was destined to take place. After the meeting, Pete took me on a tour of the facility where he introduced me to the managers and employees of the company. Some of the employees looked a little shady, but most of them seemed cool. I guess there are loud mouth trouble makers everywhere. They all respected Pete, and he seemed to know each of them personally. I could see the questions on their faces as to who I was, where I came from, how I connected with Pete, and why I wanted to work there. To them it was a mystery.

After meeting everyone, Pete showed me to the truck that I would be using for deliveries. The route was numbered 13-E. I was told it was a beast and that they had a hard time keeping a person on that route. If it was a challenge, I was up for it because I was thinking long term. I had my eyes on the prize which was part ownership; so that kept me motivated. My first couple of days at work some of my coworkers seemed to be perplexed about my style of dress and the BMW 740 IL I drove. I was supposed to be a delivery guy, not an executive. Their minds couldn't seem to put it together. I didn't realize my true blessings until they made an issue of the situation. Upper management began to question Pete about me not wearing a uniform. He readily informed them that it was my first day at work and that my uniforms were on back order. Nonetheless, all eyes were on me. They were still wondering why I was there.

My first day with training manager, Chuck, was pretty cool. He knew the delivery business inside out. He taught me the ins and outs of setting up and loading my truck and being out on the road within an hour's time. He promised to stay with me until I had the route down pat before letting me go at it alone. Chuck told me that Pete boasted about me being the man for the job. The job entailed more than I had imagined, but I couldn't have Pete and Chuck disappointed in me by not stepping up to the plate.

I gathered from our conversation that Chuck was fond of Pete because he talked about him a great deal during our training sessions. He wanted to know how well I knew Pete and to what extent. He told me that both he and Pete shared managerial responsibilities in which Pete covered the administrative duties and he covered the road and the delivery side. Chuck loved having that opportunity to get away from the building. Route thirteen was doable and it was a nice area of town. All I had to do was develop a systematic routine and the fast pace wouldn't be a problem. We arrived back at the terminal around 6:30 p.m. where we unloaded the trucks and prepared ourselves to end the day.

I made it home around 8:00 p.m. I couldn't wait to play with John. It seemed as though he had so much to show and tell me. We wrestled and chased each other around the house until we both were out of breath. John would laugh and laugh as I tickled him until his breath was gone. From the corner of my eye, I caught Sharon standing in the doorway with a satisfied smile on her face. We sat down to a wonderful family dinner to cap the evening.

I told her about my day and we laughed about some of the episodes that I shared with her. Then she went back to business as usual, asking about pay and benefits.

I could tell that Sharon was not too thrilled about me having this job because initially the pay would be low and the benefits nonexistent until an ownership position was achieved. I knew that she wanted to be taken care of. What woman doesn't want security and stability? I wanted her to see the big picture because those days were definitely on their way. I knew if I took care of her and John financially then things between us would change for the better.

It was a month before I had control of my route. I may have had to call back into the office for specific addresses or places I'd never delivered, but, for the most part. I had the route under control. As I did the job alone I saw it in a different light. It was personal for me because it was my route. It was more of a business relationship between me, the delivery driver and my customers. My image was important. When a customer or anyone should see me out and about, I was a representative of the business and right then they developed a mental picture or idea of the company. Our image, quality, and rates were our selling point. I think that I represented the company well because I was polite, hardworking, delivered on time, and knowledgeable of our services. Before long, I had the route so together that I would be able to take a four hour break. Four hours was a long time to think and be alone. I had the option to listen to all genres of music and turn it up as loud as I wanted. I loved riding through subdivisions and looking at the beautiful homes with cutting edge architectural design. I was searching for an attractive area to build a family home and I saw a few that I thought Sharon would fall in love with. That was part of the plan.

I continued to take care of Mother by making sure that she had everything she needed and that she was comfortable. She took care of me by making sure that she had a meal prepared every time I'd stop by during my lunch break. I would call her ten minutes before I arrived and she would have it piping hot on the table. That was the old school way. The good reverend wouldn't have had it any other way. After I would eat, I would take a nap for a couple of hours or some days I would just sleep if I had a long day. Sometimes I would ride around the city and enjoy the scenery just to clear my mind and think. I would think about John and my unborn baby. I would ponder thoughts about my children and giving them the best. I wanted to give them the best of love, spiritual direction, attention, education and whatever else a father could give. I wanted to give my children my time just to talk to them about whatever was on their mind and answer all the questions they might have, even the ones that don't make sense. I would think about telling them how much I loved them and how special they were and that they could accomplish anything in this world they wanted.

It didn't matter what I did or did not do, I was always the hero in John's eyes. To him, I could do no wrong. If anyone said that I did wrong, my son would say different. He believed in Daddy like everything depended on me, and it did, so I thought. I worked hard every day trying to make a better life for my family and I think Sharon saw the drive and ambition.

One day while at work it was close to lunchtime when I received a phone call from my mother. She wanted to have lunch with me. I thought maybe she was lonely or wanting to talk to me. I decided to take her to the nicest restaurant in the downtown area, Palmetto Place. During the drive, we made jokes and kidded around as usual. But a few minutes into lunch Mama's laughter began to fade. I knew she wanted to tell me something but her words had a hard time parting her lips. I couldn't understand what it could be. She was not having any problems that I knew of. She then reached into her purse and removed an envelope and slid it across the table towards me. I grew silent. I slowly opened it and to my surprise it was a check for $300,000. I was speechless. I paused for a moment and said thank you. I asked her if she was sure of giving me this amount of money even though I knew how much she had because I was the legal guardian. Of course, this was typical of my mother because she always made sure that I had more than I needed. We ate a wonderful lunch as we talked and reminisced about old times. She told me how proud she was of me being a good husband and father and taking care of her. I looked around the room to see who she was referring to.

I answered her by saying that I didn't know if I was doing as great as she thought I was, but it was not from the lack of trying. She then asked me about my recovery group and drinking. I always gave her the usual answers of 'yes, I'm going' and 'not much.' After I gave my reply, she always left me with her favorite words "stop drinking and get busy in church."

As I was backing out of the driveway from dropping my mother off, I saw Pete. I guess he wanted to chat, but

I didn't have time to chat because I was really late on my pick ups.

I rushed to the bank to deposit the check and then began my pick ups. I still finished in record time. After work, I stopped at the mall to get some gifts for my two favorite people. I bought John his favorite Thomas the Tank Engine along with a couple of toy trucks and for Sharon two beautiful bottles of Cashmere and Lauren perfumes. I know that they both would love them.

As I turned the key to open the door, I could hear the patter of John's feet running towards the door. He jumped into my arms and I swung him around in joyous greeting. I gave him a kiss and showed him the gifts I bought for him. His face lit up as he jumped up and down like it was Christmas morning. Sharon was smiling too, her eyes full of anticipation. I walked over to her doing my suave Cary Grant routine and gave her a smooth kiss on the cheek as I handed her the perfumes. Her eyes blinked in excitement - almost seductive. We made small talk about our respective days. I told her to take a hot bubble bath and relax, while I took care of John. I tucked John away in bed and returned to the bedroom with Sharon. I was relaxed and in a romantic mood and I thought she was too. But I soon realized that her mind wasn't on romance. She wanted to know if I spent the money in our account. I told her to not worry about that tonight and to enjoy the evening. I took a hot shower and got in bed. We held and rubbed and cuddled each other and before you knew it, it was morning and that meant work.

Later that day it was close to lunchtime when I received a call from Sharon. I heard the excitement in her voice. She wanted to know what was going on and why so much money was in our bank account. I told her that my mother received the insurance check from my father's passing.

My mother called and told me that Sharon thanked her for the money and showed her appreciation. During my lunch break I decided to view the houses in a lake community my cousin had referred to. It was located about twenty-five minutes from my delivery route.

I thought that this area was the ideal place to raise a family. As I drove closer to the lake community I could see over the hill top the lush green trees and shrubbery that aligned both sides of the street. The white and pink cherry blossoms and dogwoods stood at attention. I continued to the bottom of the hill and there it was sparkling in the sun like a million diamonds. A magnificent meandering lake spread away on both sides of the street.

The house lawns were neat and as elegantly manicured as a golf course. I thought that I could live like this. I came closer to the entrance of the Lake community where a tall fortress of a wall complete with security guards who stood at the entrance. I moved on through the entrance where I saw businesses, shopping stores, boutiques, salons, barbershops, karate studios, and restaurants.

It was like a little village within a city. I was amazed. Directly in the center of the intersection inside the community was this enormous three-tier circular waterfall spewing water that cascaded down the side of each circular tier. The traffic entering into this area had a great view of this colossal structure.

The homes in this area were built in the 1950's era style. Those on the lake boasted a spectacular view. I knew that Sharon would love to live here. So I visited the welcome center where they gave me brochures and website information about the many different subdivisions in the community. I took a stroll to smell the fresh air and soak in the environment and I have to say that I loved it.

I had lunch at a quaint yet elegant bistro. The atmosphere was warm, peaceful and relaxing, very cozy. I was into indulging myself so I stopped to have a drink. The waitress laughed as I placed my order for a liquid lunch. I guess she was thinking that this guy is ordering two drinks and it's barely lunch time. I had to laugh at myself as well because I was thinking the same. I soaked up the atmosphere and realized that I was still working. I figured just maybe I need to get back to work before I enjoyed this too much and forgot about my deliveries. I knew that I would be back.

I couldn't wait to get home that evening to show Sharon the glossy brochures of the lake community. I knew she would love to move there. Immediately she began to calculate what we could and could not afford but she was anxious to see the place. I called and invited my mother to join me for a visit the next day. She was more excited than Sharon and they talked all night about it.

The next day my mother saw the community and

absolutely fell in love. She instantly began purchasing items for the house, but I told her that we should wait until Sharon saw the place first. She reluctantly agreed. I took her to the bistro where I ate the day I visited. To my surprise, I had the same waitress wait on me and my mother. As she approached our table I saw a smile on her face and I knew that she remembered. She asked if I was having a liquid lunch today. Hurriedly, I said, "Water."

When the waitress went to fill our order my mother asked me what that was all about. I quickly told her that I was excited about moving into this community and that I wanted to celebrate with a drink. Then I immediately began to point out items around the community to get the focus off of me. It worked.

I took my mother home. I had one more hour to spare on my lunch break so I decided that I would go to the park, turn on my easy classical music, let my seat back and relax. Then the phone rang and it was my mother. I was just about to sink deep into my relax mode. She told me that there was a letter from my father's insurance company that said that he had a separate policy for me in the amount of a half of million dollars. After she told me that there was dead silence on the phone because I just could not believe it. I told her that I would be by after work to pick up the money, but I did not want her to tell Sharon about it.

It wasn't that I didn't want Sharon to know, but Sharon's attitude and mood changed to match fluctuations in our finances. When we had money she was the happiest person in the world. I know that we all love it when we have more and have more privileges during the good times, but what about the not so good times when we don't have money or when it is just another day. Why can't we find happiness, joy and excitement every day? I feel that affection, spontaneous reactions and sex should be great even if I didn't have $500,000 to give. Not too many people can afford to pay $500,000 for happiness. This was a great time for us and I am thankful in the good and bad times.

I was taken aback by my father putting away money for me. Maybe he was thinking about his church and me taking care of both my mother and the church. I would never know the answers; and, even though I said that I would put it to rest, I continued to ponder the realm of our relationship. My earlier indecisiveness was overruled by the desire to hurry to the bank in order to get back to work on time. I would be $500,000 richer and I didn't feel the same happiness and excitement as I felt on yesterday.

I felt I needed a drink. That lonely empty feeling of being unloved and no one understanding had crept back into my life. When I indulged in alcohol it gave me that warm feeling of being loved and held secure. I felt like I could relate to others a little better and deal with any problem that I faced. It gave me false courage and intensified my character. While under the influence, I often found myself overreacting and making bad decisions, then finding myself in difficult and awkward situations

I felt like having a drink now, but recently, I had been experiencing unusual stomach aches and today they have become worse. I hoped and prayed that it was not alcohol related. So from this day forward I will take a break from drinking. I have seriously thought about returning to Recovery class. Monday I will attend.

I had retained my Recovery Bible and other study material given to me at Recovery. I had attended AA group meetings and completed the 12 step program, but recovery deals with a spiritual perspective with the mind, body and the soul. For me the spiritual, the emotional and the physical were still too separated to make me effective in my recovery.

Hi, my name is Phillip and I am an alcoholic. I have been clean for three days. I realize that I am not God. I admit that I am powerless to control my tendency to do the wrong things and that my life is unmanageable. For it is God who restores me to sanity for his will and to act according to his good purpose (Philippians 2:13). This was my first day back at the meeting. We were encouraged to introduce ourselves only if we were comfortable doing so. My first couple of times in attendance I was reluctant. I felt powerless, truly powerless this time. I saw some new and some familiar faces. I was happy to be back. They welcomed me with open arms and big hugs along with encouragement because they knew once you've been there and done that how important it is to have the love and support. I wished everyone could attend even if they are not an alcoholic just to experience that love. It was a place of understanding and a place of safety. I attended twice a week and became more focused than ever before. I hadn't stopped drinking completely, but

I didn't drink as much.

My mother was happy for me. She believed that I would be all right. Sharon didn't say too much about it but I could tell that she was happy because she didn't have to deal with another one of my drunken episodes. She would sometimes act as if she wanted to have sex, but I often felt empty and abandoned. Weeks had passed and Sharon was still asking to see the lake community because we had some serious buyers who wanted to buy our home. I then told her about the check and she didn't believe it. Then I showed it to her. I had to calm her down because she was so upset that I waited so long to tell her.

We then got into the discussion that I was trying to avoid. I told her how I felt about the relationship over the past seven years. I told her how I felt about us not having a connection or bond. Sharon apologized for not being affectionate. She blamed it on being a mother, pregnancy, and working full-time. I told her that I had felt this way before the marriage and the kids. I told her that I wanted us to share our life together – that included hobbies, goals, and dreams. She told me that she understood and would give it a try.

That weekend Sharon and John had planned to come to Columbia on Friday after she got off of work. I made arrangements for them to meet me at a hotel in The Vista. The suite was elegant - designed as if for royalty. John played on the floor while Sharon lay on the couch watching television waiting for me to take a shower and get dressed for dinner. Everything was within walking distance of the hotel, so we strolled around to see where we would dine. We met a couple along the way and asked about a good restaurant that has a semi- family atmosphere and they referred us to John Paul. As soon as we arrived we were seated and our waitress took our order a couple of seconds later. Her first question to us was the very question Sharon despised but it was always my favorite. "What would you like to drink?" I always answered this question wrong by ordering alcohol. Sharon got an instant attitude after she heard my drink order. After that, the evening went downhill. For the rest of the evening, John and I enjoyed each other while Sharon sat in the corner like she didn't want to be there. As we left John Paul, I hoisted John on my neck and carried him for several blocks as he covered my eyes and played his favorite game of hide and seek.

Eventually we ventured into a café where the atmosphere was cozy and the seating was comfortable. There were two love seats and a nice plush sofa with a small mahogany coffee table. We sat near the large picture window and watched the people pass, disappearing into the starry night. John waved at every single person that passed by as he enjoyed his ice cream. I leaned back in the love seat and crossed my legs and sipped on one of my favorite libations, Crown Royal on the rocks. Sharon gave me her usual look of disdain. I knew that she hated my drinking and to be honest *I* hated my drinking. I wanted to stop. To anyone who has not been there it does not make sense. They would immediately say: well, stop. But it is not that easy. Some people can, some cannot. The irony was as much as she hated to see me drink I hated to see her miserable.

That night it was John and I slept in one bed while Sharon slept in the other. It seemed when she was happy I wasn't and when I was happy she couldn't be. Our happiness only intersected on special occasions. John was the first to rise that morning. Sharon made her way to the shower as if she was in a race with me. I slowly crawled out of bed because it was my day off. First things first, I had to have a cold beer. The first beer I chugged and the second I sipped. The first always hit the spot. Beer is best when iced for an entire night. We decided to get breakfast at The International House of Pancakes. After eating, we drove around taking in the sights. All the while, I had plans of taking Sharon to see the lake community. As we got closer to the community the scenery grew even more beautiful. I could tell that Sharon was becoming excited. We drove up on the hill overlooking the lake and Sharon was blown away.

We met with a realtor to discuss our plans to build a home. Sharon wanted to build right away. I played with John on the lot we had chosen while Sharon took care of business with the agent. Sharon and I decided that we wanted to be alone tonight to celebrate a little and spend some alone time together, so we decided to let John stay overnight at my mother's house.

Sharon talked about the new house all night long. I could tell that she was still excited. The next day we headed back home. After a shaky start, the weekend had turned out to be a great one. It started on shaky ground but it became better. We all were happy with a refreshed mindset and ready for the Monday morning routine. I was talking to Sharon every thirty minutes of the day. She wanted me to check on the lot where the house was being built, asking questions about the builders, the home mortgage, question after question. She called my mother about decorating. Then the process stalled and there was a waiting period. Everything was back to normal. I was still trying to make recovery meetings, but I was drinking more. I found a new hang out spot which was the Vista. My new drink was Grey Goose vodka. I felt that I needed some more excitement. Sharon and I were still missing the romance and being into each other.

Chapter 7

You Rock My World (Forbidden)

It was a clear, beautiful, sunny day and the intoxicating scent of honeysuckle was borne on the light summer breeze. Perfect I must say. I was on my route making deliveries and my next stop was an apartment complex. This complex had been under construction for a while and now it was complete. This was just what I needed more territory to cover on my route. The apartment complex was very pleasing to the eye, intriguing, although I can't say why.

Perhaps, I got the feeling that this very complex might set the course of my life in a different direction, that it might broaden my horizons and put a little steam in my step. I parked my truck and walked slowly to the entrance as I admired the lovely landscape. I entered the foyer where the open floor space was enormous so I chose the first office. I was hoping that my eyes were not deceiving me because all I saw was a set of long, tawny, beautiful legs in black pointed high heel shoes. Her hair flowed long, deep and shiny black down her back. I could smell the sweet fragrance that smelled like, happy, and it was making me weak. She turned towards me in her swivel chair and stood up, all in slow motion. I thought someone had pulled the plug on movement and sound because I couldn't speak nor hear anything. Everything went silent. She looked me in the eyes and the rich black hue of hers penetrated my soul. She was absolutely dropped dead gorgeous and perfect.

We stood before one another with straight posture as if we were sizing each other up. Then she slightly raised her left eyebrow like she had that fire. With her softly painted glossed lips and perfect white teeth, she smiled. I introduced myself and let her know that I would be taking care of the complex on my route. She then extended her hand and introduced herself as Ashley. Her silver jewelry complemented her short black skirt and champagne-colored silk blouse. She looked classy and professional.

While walking out of her office I took one last look back at her, and she was standing in place as if she was frozen. I yelled out a big yes on the inside of me. I continued on my route making deliveries and pick-ups, but everything had changed; all I could think about was Ashley. My heart was racing and my mind was at full throttle.

That night after supper I played with John until he was sleepy. I put him to bed and read to him. Seconds later he was fast asleep. I kissed him on the forehead and turned off his bedside lamp. After I took a hot shower, I checked

WENDELL PRIESTER

to see if Sharon was awake. She was sleeping like a baby. I stared into the darkness thinking about Ashley and what she was doing.

The next morning I woke up, jumped out of bed and started getting dressed to impress. My usual hour long drive seemed like fifteen minutes, maybe because I was going 100 mph. Once I arrived at work, everyone was picking on me from the time I entered the building until the time I left for my deliveries. They were wondering why I was dressed so neat and clean and smelling so good. They wanted to know if I had a special date. All I would tell them is that "this is just me and thanks for the compliment." I was glad to have my truck loaded because it was time to get on my route. Finally, I was at the apartment complex. I checked myself out one more time to make sure that everything was right then I went inside. There she was looking sweet and pretty. I slowly walked over towards her, my eyes openly admiring her as I approached.

The next day I arrived at my favorite delivery stop. I walked into Ashley's office and to my surprise she was not there. In her place was another young lady. As I was leaving the building an older lady dressed in a room service attendant's uniform approached me and said that Ashley was with a resident and I just missed her.

A few days later, Ashley and I arrived at the complex at the same time. We met at the entrance. I held the door open for her as she thanked me and invited me back into her office so that she could sign for the delivery. I told her that I missed seeing her last couple of days and offered to take her to lunch one day.

She went silent and then she reached into her desk drawer and attached her business card to my clipboard and said take care. I went back to my truck feeling a little bit better because I felt like I was making progress. We were talking more every day. We had the same sense of humor. On occasions I would sit down and get to know all the staff at the complex a bit more. Some were friendly while the others were trying to figure me out.

Mrs. Grace was hoping that Ashley and I would date. She let me know that Ashley was special and that she was fond of her. I could tell that she thought of me as being a nice guy, and I didn't want to let her down. As time went on I would ask Ashley for her home phone number. I could tell that she had someone in her life, but I was persistent. Every time I asked her she would give me her business card. So I took a break from asking her. One particular day I stopped by her office and she had balloons everywhere. Her personality was even bubblier. It was her birthday. I gave her a hug as she extended her open arms to me. She offered me cake which I thought was special. On my way out, I seriously asked her out to lunch.

I arrived exactly at eleven to pick her up, but instead she offered to drive her car. I don't know what I was thinking. I never considered the fact that she may not want to ride in a company work truck. So we rode in her new Honda Accord complete with that new car smell.

We sat in a cozy booth where she ordered a chicken tortilla. She insisted that I have a bite. Before I knew it, it was in my mouth and it tasted good. I enjoyed my baked chicken with lima beans and mashed potatoes. Ashley was killing me softly. She was very eloquent and proper yet down to earth. I found myself hanging on to every word. We had a great lunch together.

I could just imagine what dinner would be like. If it had been possible, I would have stayed with her all day. She took me back to my truck and told me how much she had enjoyed lunch. I ran to my truck to get the box wrapped in green paisley paper from the front seat. The sight of it elicited a broad smile and she delicately removed the bow and peeled back the paper. Once the box was open, she burst into a cloud of laughter and chased me through the parking lot. It was a box of her business cards which she had given me. I wrapped my arms around her shoulders as she pretended to pummel my chest. The following day I dropped by our lot to check on the progress of the house. I wanted to make sure that there were no mistakes because if there were, we would be able to detect it early and correct it. The foundation had been laid and the framing begun. The contractor rather proudly told me that they were well ahead of schedule.

Pete called and said that the company was pulling out of the contracts earlier than expected and that we need to get started on the takeover process. He explained to me that tomorrow he would have Chuck cover my route until we hire someone. There were books and books of information that I needed to learn and Pete said that we were privileged to have them before the contracts were changed and signed. He instructed me that absolutely no one else should have access to these documents and that I had to learn in a couple of days what he had learned in eight years. So I gathered all of the documents and headed for the door.

Pete informed me that on the next day I had to be prepared to handle business, which meant a suit and tie. I walked out of the office trying to be discrete, but curious eyes were watching as I made my way to my car. When I got home I immediately began reviewing the documents, but John jumped on my back, giggling. I tried to put him in front of the television, but Sponge Bob could not compete with roughhousing with Daddy. I gave in. We played until he was tired and ready for bed.

Sharon was excited about the business and the possibilities of it being successful. She wanted to make sure that the accounting part was up to par. We calculated that my projected earnings as part owner would average about $200,000 dollars annually. If this was calculated correctly, then Sharon could become the homemaker she had dreamed of becoming. And I would be the family's sole provider Sharon was beginning to trust me and my judgment. She knew very little about the business itself even after going over the documents. I myself still had questions. So I came to the conclusion that I would have to rely on Pete to explain and make sense of some of the numbers.

I told Sharon that many businesses start out like us, some are successful and some are not. I could detect the concern in her voice and in the way she twisted her mouth to one side. I reassured her that I had been a part of the start up process in a small business and it had gone well. But I was young, excited and infatuated with fast cash which allowed my business to go under. Here was an opportunity to redeem myself. After a few more hours of research I went to bed.

The next morning I awoke to see Sharon and John already dressed and ready to leave the house. It was gratifying because it was my first time being there to see them off. I went to the closet and pulled out one of my conservative suits. I'd like to think that I have a conservative taste when it comes to clothes. Appearance is everything and I got it.

Out of habit, I drove into the parking lot where the drivers were getting ready to depart on their deliveries. All eyes were on me. They saw the way I was dressed and quickly followed me back into the office to find out what was going on. They all began to shake my hand and congratulate me when they found out that I would be part owner of the company. Pete was dressed in his Sunday's best and ready to get down to business.

We signed a few contracts and conducted several business meetings until lunch time. After lunch I had to get the company business license in order and hire an accountant to set up our accounts. A mutual friend recommended his accountant of twelve years, a woman fondly called Ms. Elizabeth. She was a retired widow who knew the business inside out. Although she was undergoing treatment for uterine cancer, she readily agreed to help me set up the accounts and payroll. I was grateful to and for her because she could have refused.

All we had to do was purchase the 40 vehicles and 2 twenty-four foot trucks to get started. We projected the cost of the vehicles to be close to $700,000. We searched the entire East coast for the company that offered the best price on a fleet. Each company reminded us that we were a new company with a high risk for such a large inventory. After a few days of negotiating, Ms. Elizabeth, myself and Pete met with one of the largest fleet companies in the country. The meeting was tense as we went over the projections with a fine tooth comb. We were crunching numbers left and right until we came up with a number that was beneficial for both parties. We met with the head of the fleet company via conference call. He wanted $175,000 as down payment along with someone else with a stellar credit history and strong assets. I chose my mother to be that person.

When they saw my mother's assets and credit they patted me on the back and asked me what day and time we wanted them delivered. My mother said to me that she knew that the business would do well and she tearfully gave us her blessing.

The very next day we arranged the old trucks that were falling apart with flat tires and broken doors for pick up and made room for the new ones. Saturday morning our trucks began to arrive around 8:00am. I was at the Columbia Terminal while Pete manned the Charlotte

Terminal. They all were in place by 12 noon with brand new interiors along with driver's material and new hand trucks. On Monday morning we had a pastries and juice breakfast with our employees with juice and biscuits where we unveiled our new name, Express Enterprise Inc, and its accompanying logo. As they applauded, we handed out the keys to their new trucks. The new trucks were equipped with a keyless entry and a state of the art sound system.

After they were on the road, we drove to Charlotte to repeat the introductions, this time with pizza and soda for lunch. It felt pretty good to be President and owner of Express Enterprise Inc. with fifty-six appreciative employees. Business was going well until that Friday when the last contractor did not have the funds to pay our employees for the previous two weeks. We were not obligated to pay them, but we decided to pay the entire company in advance because most of them depended on their pay to survive. Then the billing of our fleet of trucks came in, which, though we had planned, put a dent in our operating budget.

So Ms. Elizabeth immediately made contact with the fleet dealership and told them that this bill would drive our budget into the ground. She was a tough little woman. She made reference to them as being crooks that were hiding paperwork from us and not giving us a chance to survive. Then there was silence. No one seems to know anything on their behalf. So I figured that Ms. Elizabeth's comments were accurate. She immediately went to work by asking them for a couple of days to crunch the numbers.

We all waited on pins and needles unsure of the outcome. Then we received a call from Ms. Elizabeth stating that we would be all right. I knew somehow that she would work the magical strategies that she learned over the years. I also knew that Pete and I would have to adhere to the advice of Elizabeth when it came to the budget.

———•((•))•———

Pete was responsible for accounts receivables and I was over accounts payables. We both were in constant contact with Ms. Elizabeth all day and everyday be it by phone or face-to-face. Much of our time was being spent commuting back and forth to Charlotte especially as we investigated an investment property. Since we spent many days and nights there, we needed somewhere to stay and this property would be ideal. Unfortunately, those plans fell through because of the restricted cash flow. The budget was very tight, but we were paid our normal salary, which made me assume that the business was still going well.

I finally had a chance to take a day off because our house was completed. I managed to take a walk through of the house alone because Sharon was due to have the baby any day now. I needed that time to myself, to reflect. Everything was going great. I bought Chinese food and a twelve pack and headed back to our new house. I plugged in John's television, sat on the floor and ate my green peppers and onions with beef over white rice along with my sides of egg rolls and chicken wings. I was stuffed. The first six beers seemed to magically disappear. I put the remaining six on ice. I laid back and gazed through the picture window.

Our house was on the market for about six months and we finally found a buyer; talk about perfect timing. Sharon stayed at her parents' house to prepare for the arrival of the baby. The doctors explained to us that if she did not have it within the next week then they would induce her labor. So I worked half days trying to pack and unpack and keep in touch with my managers and correspond with our corporate offices. On top of that the movers were scheduled to arrive this weekend.

Pete came and took a tour of the house. He was clearly impressed. When he was about to leave, he noticed the beer bottles and asked about my drinking. He was always concerned about me and my drinking habits because as a child Pete saw his mother's struggle with cocaine addiction. My mother and father would try to help as much as possible. Pete's father and my father were friends and they tried to intervene before it was too late. The addiction for Annalee, Pete's mom, was too overwhelming. One day Pete came home from school and found her lying face down on the kitchen table with blood streaming from her nose. He shook her lifeless body several times to awake her but got no response. Sobbing, he sprinted to our house.

When he got there I saw the look in his eyes, and I

knew exactly what was wrong. He did not have to say a word. We all rushed out of the house after my mother called the ambulance. My mother held Pete in her arms as if he were her child and told him that everything would be all right. Sometimes it was the way we were freed from the bad things that clung to our souls. Pete attended therapy for teens where he made a vow to stay away from drinking and drugs. He made me make a promise to him that I would not drink because he didn't want anything to happen to me. He felt that my family and I were the only family that he had in the world and I owed him that promise.

Life was great! The new house was coming together. My mother came over to help arrange the furniture and put her special touch on the decorating. She even ordered custom window treatments. The hardwood floors sparkled like glass as she placed the oriental rugs to offset the rooms' flow. My mother was a professional. The colors we chose blended well with the flower arrangements and accessories she chose. From the landscape, to the precisely manicured lawn, to the pine straw flower beds, everything was well coordinated. We were set. For the time being I was living as a bachelor. Sharon and John stayed at her mother's because she did not want to bring our new born baby Allen home yet. She planned to submit her two weeks' notice at her job to devote her time in raising the children, but she delayed making her resignation final because we needed her insurance.

Express Enterprise was doing very well. We had the

best service numbers in the region. An email was sent out from our corporate office to all the contractors stating that Express Enterprise was ranked number one. We shared that good news with our employees and provided them with an employee appreciation breakfast. The accomplishment had been that of the team.

The majority of the employees seemed proud of the accomplishment except Chuck. We'd notice a change in his attitude and his job performance. He no longer gave 100% percent and his outlook appeared negative. The rest of the team noticed and began to avoid contact with him. Then the real reason for his personality change was revealed. I approached him to discuss some changes for that day's schedule, and he complained to me that he felt that he had been overlooked although he had been the one who kept the company going. I explained that being an owner requires more than running a route or even managing the operation. I let him know that if he had a problem working for us then maybe he should start looking elsewhere for employment. We had an obligation to our customers to provide a quality service. And his name wasn't on anything. I promptly went to have a short meeting with Pete.

Pete agreed with what I had told Chuck and suggested we begin a search to replace him. Ms. Elizabeth wanted us to fire him immediately because she felt that we did not need a snake in management. In the end, news swirled that we were replacing managers one by one and we did. Chuck got wind of it and quickly changed his attitude.

Business and the operations were running smoothly. Pete began having car problems and my BMW was an older model and we both needed dependable cars to commute back and forth between Charlotte and Columbia. So Pete purchased a sleek grey-toned Suburban and I upgraded to a brand new seven series under the company's name so that we could use it as a tax write off. Pete and I were doing better financially than we could have ever imagined.

I headed back to spend time with my family. When I drove into my in-law's yard, Sharon skipped from the porch with a surprised look on her face. She loved the car. John wanted to take a ride so we all went out for dinner including Sharon's parents. The food was good and the company amiable. I told her parents that it was time that Sharon and the boys came home, and they agreed without a fuss I guess Sharon and the boys missed me as much as I missed them.

Sharon and I spent quality time until the late hours of the night, and I really enjoyed it. The entire weekend was wonderful. After church on Sunday we cooked out on the grill, and John and I played ball together. He had so much to talk about. He didn't stop talking until it was bedtime when I read him a new bedtime story. And he fell fast asleep in the middle of Who Is that Funny Bunny. Before bed that night Sharon confided that she was ready to move into the new house. She felt that this would be a good time because John would be out of school in a month for summer break. The next morning I left for work early.

I wanted to focus on the operation to make sure we maintain that level of excellence. Also to keep an eye on our investment, Pete informed me that he received a request to take on more contracts.

Another station was opening in the Charlotte area and we were at the top of the list for the contract because of our excellent service performance numbers. Once the drivers were loaded and on the road, the managers who did not have to go on the road remained in the building to make sure that the warehouse was cleaned and everything accounted for. Then they would watch the computer screens to make sure that our service commitments were made.

At least twice a week I would tee off at 10:00 a.m. or I would take my boat out to the lake. I enjoyed the fresh morning smell and the early morning sunshine. I was an average player who didn't like to get into too much competition. I really enjoyed the game and the ambiance. After the game I visited Ashley. As I pulled in the parking lot she was riding towards me in a golf cart. I could tell that she did not recognize who I was until she had gotten closer and I got out of my car. She smiled as she walked towards me while asking if it was mine.

I invited her out to lunch. I opened her door for her like a true gentleman and everyone watched as we backed out of the complex. They waved as if they wanted us to see that they saw everything. I was listening to John Mayer, one of her favorite artists. She was still amazed. She couldn't believe what her eyes were seeing.

We then pulled up to The Motor Supply Co. Restaurant where a valet opened her door and then mine. We walked in and I could see the smile on her face as if she was very pleased. I knew I had her then. Instantly my two way pager went off and it was one of my managers giving me an update on our service.

I turned to her, "Enough about me. It seems as though you have the world on your shoulders. What about you? How is life treating you?" She took a deep breath and as she was getting ready to speak our waiter came and asked for our drink order. Ashley ordered water and I order a bottle of chilled Riesling wine. We both had a fresh garden salad and their famous crab cakes. I wanted to finish the conversation.

Time was flying, lunch was almost over and Ashley only had an hour to spare. So I asked her if she would like to hangout this evening and maybe I could cheer her up. She agreed. I stopped by the Columbia terminal to check on the operation and everything was quiet. I made contact with Pete in the Charlotte terminal and he was in the operation. Pete loved hands on and being directly involved in the day to day operations, which is in essence, micromanagement. He always made joke about me playing golf instead of working and we laughed about it.

On Pete's advice I took off for the day since the operations were running smoothly in Columbia and Charlotte. I went home and took a hot shower. As I sipped on Grey Goose with a splash of pineapple (in the shower!), I listened to a mellow slow groove. . I got out of the shower and slowly dried my body in front of the opened blind window as I admired the trees and all nature around me. It was nice not to have neighbors, especially today. It was the month of May in South Carolina and it already felt like summertime. I threw on a polo shirt with a pair of seersucker pants, a palmetto belt, a pair of loafers and my best cologne.

I started up the BMW, opened the garage door and slipped on my favorite pair of shades. I rolled back the sunroof and I was off. I cruised down the boulevard listening to a selection from Bob Marley. Many people were on the strip walking, jogging and riding their bikes. Kids played on the sidewalk. I arrived at Ashley's place about five minutes early and parked beside her car. She stepped out of her place towards her car but didn't notice me until I rolled my window down and asked if she wanted a ride. At first she looked startled, but as recognition sank in she gave me a beautiful smile. She got into my car to start the evening.

We rode around for awhile listening to Bob Marley. She was enjoying the music, the scenery and the ride. I stared directly into her eyes without a smile and she into mine. She stared long enough to let me know that she understood that I wanted her. Then she slowly looked away and gazed out the window at the scenery. We arrived at The Blue Marlin restaurant, where we dined outside and ate without talking or rushing.

I just wanted to be alone with her. As we were leaving the Blue Marlin I asked her if she wanted to stop at my place since I had been to hers. She agreed. We approached the hill overlooking the lake and she was blown away by its beauty. Once we entered the subdivision, she was even more amazed. She saw all the people and the shops and made mention that the Harbison area was nothing like it. I pulled into my driveway and let the garage door up midway and drove through. I turned the alarm off and walked inside. I did not offer a seat because I wanted to see what she was going to do. I walked through the house closing all the window blinds. When I returned she was still standing. I asked her if she was cold because I saw her rubbing her arms as if she wanted the blood to circulate a little bit better.

I then wrapped a throw around her shoulders while hugging her with warmth. I lit the fireplace to knock the chill off the room and to set the mood. Soon the room was bathed in the glow of dancing firelight and the pungent smell of wood smoke. I complimented her on her outfit. She was wearing a pair of nicely fitting khaki shorts along with a form fitting halter top accented. Pink toenails peeked from handmade leather sandals. She was gorgeous in the simple things.

We sat in front of the fireplace admiring the room and talking for hours about everything under the sun, from our religious beliefs, politics, family, relationships to the pleasures of the ear and the pleasures of the tongue. We couldn't believe how much we had in common and we connected like soul mates. The feeling was thrilling and scary at the same time. We covered more ground in one day than some people share in a lifetime.

Ashley talked about her mother and father as she remembered them when she was younger. She recalled their frequent, late-night arguments, the degradation that her father heaped out. Her father blamed his violent behavior on the Vietnam War. Eventually, he walked out on them, leaving their mother to make a multitude of sacrifices so that they would have the basic necessities like clothing, food and shelter. She made sure that they knew of God and His mercy. She kept them in church. I told her about my father, about how we never truly connected. Then moving to lighter topics, I mentioned playing the drums and I found out that she played the acoustic guitar.

The evening was great with her. It was getting late and she kidded me that some people have to go to work. She wanted to take a tour of the house before leaving. When we came upon my boys' room, she asked about them and their mother. I played it off as we were not together.

We both were feeling pretty nice at this point, but it was time to go. We got into the car and I changed the music. For some strange reason I wanted to listen to some rap music so I popped in Jay-Z and then I played TI. She bobbed her head to the beat. It became obvious that she appreciated music from classical to rap. I got on the interstate and opened the Beamer up. I let her feel the power. She held on tight as she smiled and seemed to be down for whatever, and I liked that.

I walked Ashley to her door but she didn't let me in.

She said that her place was in a horrible mess. So she gave me a hug and a little kiss good night. I cruised back home, washed the glasses, cleaned the house and went to sleep. Ashley had good morals and integrity. She seemed too good to be true.

It was time for Sharon and the boys to come home, so I took the company twenty-footer to pick up the rest of the furniture. John rode with me in the truck and Sharon and Allen followed in the car. We got to the house and I opened the back gate to let John in and he saw his new sand box and wood tower swing set. Sharon held Allen as she watched John play. As I unloaded the furniture, I paused for a moment to look out back at my family. I saw such beautiful, excited, smiling faces. The picture was almost perfect. And I thought to myself that this was how it was supposed to be. I called Pete to meet me at the Terminal to return the truck.

I raced to get back home to be with my family. Looking at John play and seeing. Allen kicking and shouting with excitement, I began to realize how fast time flies. Just yesterday I could remember hearing John cry for his bottle. I also could remember my own imagination of make-believe people. Sometimes, I would pick up a toy air plane or drive a toy race car and play with my star wars action figures. John would smile shame faced wondering how I knew what was going on in their world. It was just yesterday when I had been there myself.

Sharon and I were getting along better. We had become good friends when it came to the children but we still led largely separate lives. We were a study in discussions and connecting briefly at a distance. To deal with our problems or issues was to have a fight and then run back to our corners and come back out fighting again only to make things worse. Sadly, we sat on the sidelines watching our lives drift away.

Ms. Elizabeth called Pete and me on a three way conference call and informed us that the business was not going as planned. The truck payments were eating up our cash flow, and we were getting behind on payroll. She said that she was aware of the other contracts we were scheduled to pick up in the near future, but until we get more revenue we needed to make some cuts In the meantime, she wrote a proposal to the IRS describing our strategy for catching up and becoming current on taxes again. .

Ms. Elizabeth has been in the corporate world over thirty years and she has dealt with business lawyers, other accountants and the IRS. She had a weird sense of humor but she got the job done.

Later that evening, I met up with Ashley. Before coming over, I picked up some Chinese food, movies and beer. I gave her an hour, and then I knocked at the door. She opened the door and stood before me wearing a short robe and I could tell there was with nothing under it. Her hair was dripping wet from the shower. She gently patted it dry with a lush towel. She stepped back from the entrance. At that moment I wanted to hold and caress her in my arms. She appeared to be a tenderness young lady in the world calling out to be loved in a romantic way. I wanted to overpower her with my sweet passion. I had to tell myself, "Phillip, hold your horses and take your time in a gentle way because everything that you've built from the moment you both first met like trust, respect, humor and passion could be lost by your one false move." I restrained myself. I handed her the movies and placed a beer for her and I on the table coasters. The other beer went into the freezer. She invited me to take a shower and I did. The hot shower went very well with the cold beer. She asked if I had seen any of the three movies that I rented which were *Serendipity*, *Finding Forrester*, and *Frankie and Johnny*. I had seen Frankie and Johnny but not the others. We decided to watch the others first. Ashley, like me, was a movie fanatic.

After drinking a twelve pack, devouring all the boxes of Chinese food and watching three movies we ended up in bed. I awoke the next morning not remembering the going to sleep part. I looked at the clock and it was two hours before I had to report to work. I woke Ashley and in her sleepy sexy voice she said," Okay," and walked me to the door, asking for a hug. I obliged and simultaneously caressed her backside. I didn't want to rush and I didn't want to leave, so I asked her if she wanted me to stay. She softly pounded on my chest with her fist and laughed as she called me a pervert. I went home to take a quick shower. When I got there Sharon and the boys were eating breakfast. Sharon made a snide remark about having assumed that I was in Charlotte. She hadn't expected me to be here for John's first day of school. Little did she know that I wouldn't have missed it for the world.

After breakfast, we walked John to his classroom, a world of miniatures with colorful signs and tags everywhere. With the teacher's help, John put his book bag in his little cubbyhole and sat at his desk. When it was time for us to leave, I almost cried because our baby was growing up. He waved goodbye as we stopped outside of the classroom peeped back in. There were other parents standing along with us. Some were crying and others were rushing off to work. Sharon went back home and I went to work.

Our corporate office wanted to talk to Pete and myself about starting the new contract in Charlotte. That means twenty-six more employees in Charlotte and ten more in Columbia. We had to take over the airport operations in both cities I asked that we meet on tomorrow to discuss it further and they all agreed. I picked up John after school and he was so excited. I told him to slow down before he burst something. He was talking almost one hundred miles per minute. He had so much to tell me all I could do was listen.

I called Ashley and we talked about our evening. She said that her time with me was warm and relaxing. She told me that it felt as though she had known me all of her life because she felt safe and comfortable with me. She went on to tell me that I had a good heart and also was a very sexy dad. She wanted to get together again soon. I told her that we would, but I would be tied up in meetings for the next couple of days.

Pete and I entered the new terminal office to meet with the managers as they were expecting us. We gave them the history of our company and the philosophy of our operation. Then we proceeded to get down to business. First on the agenda were employee's salaries including management, and then driver routes responsibilities. Second was a walk through to meet the drivers. Of course, they were curious as to who we were and what kind of owners we were. Some seem skeptical due to our youth. Others had a few smart comments—like that was a good way to start off with new owners. I asked Clarence who was one of our managers from the first Charlotte terminal if there were any troublemakers. He assured me that there were a couple of wannabes but they were harmless. Our first Charlotte terminal had more hard characters than Sing Sing. Clarence could switch from a professional to a thug mentality at a moment's notice. I could tell that there was more involved there than Express Enterprise. Some of the cars the employees drove were more than double their salaries. The convictions on their criminal records said it all. But we overlooked their past and they respected us. With adding on this new terminal in Charlotte, most of my time would need to be there and Clarence was the man I would definitely need to get close to. For the next couple of days we went over the numbers to determine what it would take to run this terminal. After Ms. Elizabeth and corporate came up with a figure that we all could agree upon, we signed on the dotted line. We had many meetings and I was in Charlotte at least three days or more out of the week, but still I juggled the time to see my family and Ashley.

Two things you can't hide and those are love and money. Business now was stable. The family was great. Ashley and I went out to eat at the Hunters Gatherer restaurant on the university campus where there was live music. This particular night they invited musicians and vocalists to come up and give an impromptu performance. After a number of drinks, I dared Ashley to go and play the guitar. She said that she would if I would play the drums. We both went on stage as the M.C. announced us and everybody applauded. Ashley then faced me with her back to the audience with a huge smile on her face. I was laughing as I was adjusting the drums. I asked her if she was ready and she gave me a nod, yes. I began to play a nice funky groove as she chimed in with a smooth rhythm and blues. It was our first time playing together and it felt like we had been together for years. We made beautiful music together, the kind of music that elicits movement from the stiffest of audience members. Our performance ended with a standing ovation. After a couple more drinks we offered to pay the tab, appreciative audience members insisted on paying it. On that note we left. We walked down the sidewalk swaying from side to side as we kissed, hugged and laughed trying to hold each other up from falling. We finally made our way to the car.

As I drove away she was kissing all over me. I was trying to focus but it was hard to resist. We got out of the car still entangled with each other. I threw her up against the wall where we melted together; we couldn't get enough of each other. We made our way up to her apartment where we fell inside while taking each other's clothes off. We were locked together like two magnets crawling to the bedroom. Ashley's hoarse whisper in my ear was that she wanted me - enflamed me. I gently picked her up in my arms like a baby and laid her on the bed. A trail of clothes ran from the front door to the bed. My body against hers played a beautiful melody once again. She wrapped herself around me as we danced to a sexual rhythm that was like a drumbeat as I pounded with aggressive, yet gentle, passion. She sang a soothing ballad so soft and sensual until our bodies sweated and trembled with need. After a climax that was shattering, we collapsed in ecstasy holding each other close as sleep enveloped us. I awoke the next morning to Ashley staring me in the face. I opened my eyes as she gave me a big smile. She then covered her face in a pillow and screamed. I tickled her as she jumped out of bed and ran to the bathroom. I watched her as she turned on the shower and combed her hair in the mirror. I stared at her beautifully sculptured body, so perfectly shaped, like an hour glass. I didn't want to leave her, but it was her weekend to work. She told me that she was tired of working at the complex. I took a shower and headed home.

The boys were glad to see me. I picked them up kissed them and tickled them all over. Sharon left the kids with me so that she could run errands. I took John and Allen into the backyard and played every game we could think of. We played football, soccer, basketball and every ball there is. The game they enjoyed the most was chase. I chased them all over the yard until I was tired. John would knock Allen down trying to get away. Poor Allen could barely walk but he was determined to run. A few hours later they were as worn out as I was. We settled in for a nap together. It was refreshing to be outdoors with them and I enjoyed every minute of it. Sharon brought the chicken and beer back that I asked for the family cookout. I fired up the grill with chicken, and potatoes and all the other fixings. I thought about Ashley before Sharon got back and gave her a call. I told her that I was spending time with my boys while she was stuck in the office at work on this beautiful spring like day in September. She wasn't too thrilled about that. Sharon, the boys and I ate out on the back deck until we all were stuffed. We had enough food left over that there would be plenty for Sunday dinner. The day was beginning to wind down as I watched the kids play in their sand box. I sipped on a cold beer. After putting the kids to bed, I showered and got into bed. I lay in bed next to Sharon staring at the ceiling thinking about Ashley and what she was doing.

It was Sunday morning and we were invited to the church where I attended my recovery sessions. The greetings of the members were warm and welcoming. We were invited many times before but this time we elected to go because we needed a church home. I saw a few people who attended recovery as I did. In their Sunday best, they appeared immune to struggles like addiction. The pastor began to deliver his message and he had my attention instantly. He talked about how we all have difficulties in our lives that cloud our judgment. I thought that no one else in the world could be having the same struggles as me. I thought that I was the only one. It is funny how we think that it is all about us. I don't know how the pastor knew to speak on that subject on the day I attended his church, but I don't think that it was a coincidence.

We ventured out to the park after services - this had become our family tradition on Sunday afternoons. The park was filled with children playing, parents watching, friends in fellowship and lovers holding hands. What a way to end the day. I was relaxed and content for the moment.

That Monday morning I arrived at the first Charlotte terminal at approximately 6 a.m., around loading time. The trucks were loaded and out of the building in no time. I talked with Clarence just to get to know him a little bit more. From how he conducted business, I surmised that he was a stand up kind a guy. He gave me a thorough tour, narrating the tour with the kind of information that I needed. We shook hands and I was gone for the day. I gassed up, brought a six pack, and got on Interstate 77 while listening to the Yellow Jackets. My phone rang and it was Ashley.

I drove straight to her job. As soon as I walked in and she immediately excused herself from her clients and rushed to me with a big hug and a kiss like she wanted me right then and there. She whispered in my ear that her clients were rude and obnoxious and getting on her nerves.

I told her that I would wait for her at the apartment until she finished up with her clients. Ashley came to the apartment while I was taking a shower where she joined me. She washed my body as I washed hers. We toweled off and lay in bed. I took my time and slowly kissed her entire body until she could not resist. She started to scream as she pulled the silk sheets with passion while pushing my head away all in one motion. It was like the first time all over again. We cuddled together shivering and panting uncontrollably. Then we both burst into laughter. We didn't know why. We had lost track of time and Ashley had to get back to work. I drove away thinking about her and only her.

Thirty minutes into my drive my phone rang and it was Ashley. She told me that she had quit her job because she couldn't take it anymore. She also told me how the sex between us was incredible. She couldn't stop her legs from quivering. She then demanded that I come and get her.

———

I picked her up, and she decided that she wanted to do something spontaneous. That spontaneous day meant a day in Savannah, Georgia. Ashley knew of a nice cozy restaurant there that we might like so we hit the road. The joy I saw in her eyes pulled me in and I was happy.

The restaurant was an English Tudor style cottage but modern. The cozy atmosphere titillated our senses and made us want each other even more. We had an elegant dinner with drinks that rivaled no other. The Peking duck was cooked to perfection. We fed each other as if we were newlyweds. And the guests fed into the idea as they commented on our young love. Ashley elected to drive back but fifteen minutes into the drive she couldn't handle it. I ended up behind the wheel all the way from Savannah.

The new contracts increased the salaries for Pete and me by $50,000 a year. We hired a new regional manager and a maintenance guy from outside of the company. The Regional Manager's position was being pursued by all of our terminal mangers, but we decided to hire from outside the company. This was Pete's idea. I didn't quite understand why but I supported his decision because we were partners.

The added position decreased my workload considerably. I would meet with our managers once a week by conference call from my house, the terminal or from Ashley's place. Nobody needed to know my location unless there was a problem or they needed help. Sometimes I would help in the operations during the early mornings or in the evenings.

I made it to recovery, although not frequently. One Tuesday I arrived just in time for the inspiration section. And it's been a while since I've been able to make it, not that I didn't want to. They were still introducing methods of inspiration and one read:

"You"
I'm sorry for the things I've done
And I told you that I wouldn't do them again.
You said to me your promises are true.
Your grace and mercy for ever endure.
The moment I try and do good sin is there
To trip me up, but then all I need from you is
One simple touch...
My freedom of love I pursue...
The love of freedom I have in you.

Chapter 8
Integrity

E arlier that day I went to my mother's house and took my father's clerical collar shirt and hat without permission. If she had known the reason I took the shirt and collar she would kill me. It was Halloween and I wanted it to be my costume. Sharon and I took the children to our church to participate in the festivities as opposed to going door to door. When we returned home, I told Sharon that we were having a get together with some of the company employees. The truth was that the Reverend for the evening was going to meet Ashley at one of her ex co-worker's costume party. Ashley was to dress up like Cat Woman. I know; what a couple! We entered the party and everyone was both thrilled and surprised to see Ashley. While they were catching up on old times, I talked with the guys and had some drinks. I overheard the ladies asking questions about me. I saw Ashley laughing. I guess I was convincing wearing all the black including a white reverend collar.

We had fun that night until we left the party. For some

strange reason Ashley didn't want to go to her place that night. She asked that we go to my house instead. I told her that we couldn't go to my house tonight because my family was there. I then had to tell her what I had been dreading for a long time. I told her about Sharon and our "situation". She was furious. She said that she thought that I was separated, not married because if she knew that she would not have gotten involved with me.

She released a sigh of frustration as she propped her elbow on the window sill and rested her head in the palm of that hand. She stared out the window into the darkness in silence. I knew that this moment would come, but I didn't know that it would come to an end. I didn't know what was going to happen. I felt empty inside. I knew that I was wrong and I was only thinking of myself and what I wanted. I brought this situation to her only to cause her pain. I was thinking if she only knew who I was and if she got to know me I think she would be very fond of me. All I needed was a little of her time and possibly sex then I knew she couldn't resist even when she found out I was married. Now I know that she hates me and I can't blame her. Crazy as it may sound I would do it all over again. I knew I had to make a decision, but I simply couldn't.

We reached her apartment and before the car was in park Ashley was out the door and strutting up the pathway. I ran after her, but she put up her hand without looking in my direction. I knew that meant for me not to come any further. For all it was worth I said that I was sorry, but what was I sorry about? I waited until she got inside, then

I drove away. She did not answer my repeated attempts to phone her.

The more I thought about it the worst I felt. Early on I had sensed that Ashley was a woman of integrity. I wasn't going to make contact with her ever again. Perhaps, I needed to find some integrity of my own. The next day I visited the Charlotte terminal. I wanted to remain busy and spend more time with the business and my family. I wanted to keep my mind occupied. After the drivers were on the road Clarence and I grabbed a bite to eat and had a few drinks at Spinnakers. He seemed amazed to have caught me in a relaxed mood. I knew that he could handle himself well. After we left the mall we drove around Charlotte sightseeing. We talked and found out that we had a lot in common. I figured he was cool.

He was still handling business on his two-way as we rode around. He knew every driver's route and every stop. The guy was sharp. He said that he needed to get back to the terminal to make sure that everything is still running smooth and I respected that.

On my way home I called Sharon and we talked about the boys and what was generally going on. I suggested that we were long overdue for a vacation. I stopped at the store and picked up a six pack. Sharon ordered Papa John's pizza while I wrestled and played with the boys. I gave them their baths and brushed their teeth as they looked in the mirror smiling. I was looking at more than just their teeth. I was looking at their eyes, their hair, nose and ears in a search for the traits that they have from me, my parents and Sharon. I longed each day to see the development of their personalities. They loved a good tickling before bed along with a story. After that I would give them a kiss and tucked them away.

I walked into the bedroom where Sharon was wearing a golden, shimmery silk nightgown. She had cut her hair in a bob which framed her face in an almost sexy way. I thought that was sweet that she was having a moment. I guess talking about a vacation and spending family time may have sparked the feeling. So I took a shower and put on a splash of smell good. I got in bed and we caressed each other as I kissed her briefly. Then we had sex. Instead of cuddling afterwards, she rose with very little emotion and tiptoed into the bathroom. The shower immediately came on. A few minutes later she emerged smelling of Dove with her hair wrapped in a satin scarf. In no time, she was fast asleep. I shook my head and smiled.

I couldn't stop thinking about Ashley. I wanted so much to talk to her. I never meant to hurt her. I just had not thought things through. I checked my voice mail every day to see if she had called. Every time the phone rang I wished it was her. It has been several weeks now and still no word. Paul Howard took the headphones off and sat back in his chair. He was emotionally drained by what he had heard so far. He needed a drink of water and a brief respite before he got back into the story. About ten minutes later he sat down, put the headphones on and switched the recorder back on. He prepared himself for whatever ending would come to this man he had come to admire.

Thanksgiving Day we served dinner for the family at our home. After the feast, which included both a roasted turkey and a fried one, a baked ham ringed with pine-apple slices, dressing, gravy, rice, potato salad, macaroni and cheese, yams, pound cake, and sweet potato pie, we all sat around talking and receiving phone calls from well wishers. Pete and I stepped out of the room to shoot the breeze when I received a phone call and it was Ashley. Pete looked at me with a raise of the eyebrow that I pretended not to notice.

Ashley wished me a happy Thanksgiving and then she went on to tell me how she felt about things between us. She told me that she was overwhelmed and frustrated be-cause her feelings for me ran deep. She also said that she tried walking away from me, but she couldn't bring herself to do it. She said that she didn't believe in adultery, but she wanted to talk things over with me the next day.

I met Ashley at her mailbox on Thursday at 11:00 o'clock AM, right around the time she received her un-employment checks. I pulled up beside her and asked her if she needed a ride. She told me that she did not ride with strangers as she gave me a sexy smile and got in. Trembling, I reached for her hand. She looked into my eyes briefly then looked away. The wind was blow-ing her hair in her eyes and mouth. She squinted her sad somber eyes, and I could tell that she was still hurting and disappointed. We headed to her apartment and immediately she began to vent.

She told me that she was compromising her beliefs if she stayed in the relationship with me. I told her that I felt the same, but if it weren't for my boys then I would have been ended the relationship with Sharon. I told her that I was not in love with Sharon. Ashley came to the conclusion that she would wait for me but only for a year. She was allowing me enough time to get the divorce proceedings started. I kissed her and that led to us making out.

She was so happy she must have temporarily forgotten that I was a married man. This was perfect timing, the holiday season. Christmas concerts at the Koger Center for the Performing Arts were always spectacular. The symphony with musical bells and choirs singing Christmas carols amazed as usual. In the middle of the Christmas rush, she agreed to accompany me to the Philharmonic Christmas concert. She was shocked to see me arrive at her front door in a stretch limo. I already had the drinks on ice awaiting her arrival. She was wearing a sleek black elegant skirt with a soft white silk blouse accented with a double strand of pearls. Her ears sparkled with a pair of diamond earrings. Her hair lay softly over her eye. Her long legs were elegant perfection in sheer satiny black panty hose. She was flawless. I was holding my own. I wore an elegant black tuxedo with a clean shave and Desire cologne. That's all I needed. We had many compliments that evening. I think that we made a fashion statement. The concert was outstanding. All of the performances were great. Immediately after the concert we met and mingled with the musicians over a glass of wine. Ashley and I painted the town getting tipsy in the back of the limo.

The mood was right so I began kissing her and she dropped her wine glass to the floor. When I unbuttoned her blouse and began kissing her breasts, we lowered ourselves to the floor as, breathlessly, we began to undress each other. She lay before me in only her pearls and heels. With the sunroof open, we made love under the stars. We awoke to sound of the limo driver tapping on the window. I instructed him to take us home to her place When we arrived he opened the door and I handed him a crisp $100 dollar bill and thanked him for the evening. Free of interruptions, we spent the rest of the day cuddling in her apartment.

Sea Island Resort eleven miles……..

When we finally resurfaced, we drove the two hours from Columbia to Brunswick, Georgia, a thriving waterfront city. The ride was relaxing and enjoyable. Sharon seemed relaxed and comfortable as we listened to Jill Scott and Rachelle Ferrell. No begging, apologizing and no phone calls. It was just a peaceful ride. The countryside and all of nature seemed intent on pleasing our senses. The boys slept.

We finally arrived at the entrance to Sea Island where the guard checked our reservation. This island had heavy security because of its high profile celebrity clientele. The last time we visited we saw John Travolta. President George Bush was also a frequent visitor. We kept straight at a slow pace while admiring the beautiful scenery. The enormous oak trees and winter green grass danced with the colorful array of flowers. The pampering started as soon as we arrived. Our car doors were opened. They greeted us with welcome cocktails at the lobby as we checked in at the front desk.

Our room keys were issued to us along with our Sea Island credit card and a resort map which they made sure we knew how to use it properly. The Sea Island credit card is issued because cash is not used anywhere on the island. The doorman then ushered us off to where our chauffeur awaited to take us to our suite. If we needed to go anywhere all we had to do was call. So we made arrangements for dinner. The meals were gourmet and outstanding, the best I've ever had. We lavished ourselves with everything from massages and facials to golf and tennis.

Sharon and I had reservations for brunch so I rushed back to take a shower and get dressed. As I dressed, we sipped on some drinks of amaretto sour and vodka and cranberry juice. The latter was my favorite. It was fifty-nine degrees on Christmas Eve and it was absolutely beautiful.

We had an oceanfront suite with sliding glass doors that we kept open the majority of the time. Beyond those doors lay an ocean that shimmered as if diamonds floated on the surface. After brunch we took the boys for a walk on the beach. Riding our rented bikes all over the island we recorded every move we made. The historical homes were gorgeous. I would definitely purchase a home there if I had the funds. We brought the boys back to take a nap;

surprisingly they welcomed the rest.

Our dinner reservation was scheduled for 6:00 where there would be a seven course meal. We were elegantly dressed. Sharon wore a formal gown in fuchsia: I wore a black tuxedo accented with a bow tie; and the boys wore Ralph Lauren plaid pants with blue blazers. I thought that we were the best dressed family in the place.

Down the hall they were playing a mixture of classical music and oldies. So we decided to venture in. We shagged and waltzed to the beat, and then my boys took the floor. I don't know what they were doing, but they were moving with confidence. I didn't get a chance to dance with Sharon because of the boys. We had to be back at our suite by 8:00 so we left. The chauffeur was waiting in a black Lincoln to drive us back.

The Christmas lights adorned every possible venue and were everywhere, done with a professional flair that was breathtaking. We got to the room and gave the boys a bath and put them in their pajamas. Then the doorbell rang and it was Santa and his elves with cookies, milk and hot chocolate. The elves sang Christmas carols, told the boys a bedtime story and tucked them in bed. The boys were not expecting that to happen.

The last day of our winter vacation we made plans to shop and visit the sites for the last time. After eating dinner we took the boys to the movies to see Robots. John was becoming a movie fanatic much like me. As we took our seats, John told me that we were buddies and that he loved it when I took him to movies. He held my hand jumping up and down. He was so excited. John asked if my dad took me to the movies when I was a little boy too. I tried to avoid the question, but John was persistent. I told him that he didn't and then I knew the next question was going to be why not.

Silenced and frozen in place I reflected back to the kid in me because I used to ask my mother the same questions. I thought that the older I became that part of me would fade away, but it seemed to get worse because of my relationship with my boys. Our relationship only reminded me of my own estrangement from my father. Why? The theatre went dark as the tears rolled down my face.

The brief ride home still allowed time for reflection on my decisions about everyone in my life including my relationships with both Sharon and Ashley. I needed to focus on the positive, things that were within my power to change. I needed to pray and hope that my life got better. I needed to stay strong until it did. Two hours of pondering, and we were back at home. After a good night of rest, I started feeling more responsible. That was one of my positive outlooks.

Sharon and I went to the insurance company and purchased a one million dollar life insurance policy. If anything should happen to her or me the children would be financially stable for awhile. I took Sharon back home and I went to work. I walked into the terminal and noticed freight left behind and a couple of trucks parked. Not a good sign. I immediately went to management and asked what was going on. Two employees had childcare issues.

The others walked off the job because they did not receive their checks. I quickly called Pete in Charlotte to see if he knew about the situation in the Columbia terminal. He knew about it because the same thing was happening in the Charlotte terminal as well. I asked him why he didn't contact me. Even though I was on vacation I needed to know. He said that I couldn't do anything. Pete said that he had tried to get in touch with Ms. Elizabeth but had discovered that she was in the hospital and wasn't able to be disturbed. I went to the bank and made sure that money was in the payroll accounts to pay the employees who had not been paid. It was. Service was shot for the day, though, but we would make it up tomorrow. I apologized for the mishap. Some understood and realized that we would come through for them while the others complained. Ironically, the ones who complained were the ones who routinely requested advances and needed to use the trucks every now and then but business is business.

After spending some time in operations things seemed to be running smoothly. Elizabeth was now home recuperating from the operation. She was in constant contact with payroll, the business insurance, and with payroll taxes. I was in Charlotte the majority of the time. It was much more to keep an eye on.

One morning there was a surprise visit by the feds, totally unexpected. It was a total of five of them wearing plain clothes. They were not speaking a word to anyone. I knew what was going on because I had seen them in the Columbia Terminal but this was something new to these guys as far as happening on the job. I didn't want them to become alarmed so as they were making their way through the terminal with corporate I spoke to a few individuals to reassure them that I was fully at ease with what was going on. There was contraband shipped through delivery companies every day. Some they caught, especially if they had an inside track. Clarence came to me pointing and talking about freight issues. He asked me if I knew anything about the Fed's visit. I told him that I was just as surprised as they were but that I didn't expect any negative outcomes.

The drivers were on the road so I called Pete to come over to the First Charlotte terminal, but contracts and the Feds had already called me into the office. They had been watching the operations and had suspicions but were unable to track down certain suspects because of an inside connection. They wanted the names of everybody who was responsible for verifying shipping and receiving. I told them who we had working on the night shift along with our supervisors. It was a huge operation to pinpoint an individual especially someone inside. We had to be careful with our suspicions and to make sure they couldn't hold our company responsible. We did have access to the airplanes which posed the biggest problem area for contraband. The problem was packages were not being registered and were being shuttled through the system without tracking numbers. By the questions they were asking and the attention they were giving me I knew that they thought it was me or at least I knew who had the access to do so. I knew that even after they left they would be watching.

Clarence treated me to a late lunch. We ate and had a few drinks. I knew that he wanted to talk about something other than business. We came close once before to talk about that subject but never did. So out of respect we didn't cross the line. But now there was a need to cross it. I extended my hand and said, "If you know anyone or anything about the packages, I need to know if anything is going on."

He shook my hand and said, "Nothing is going on." On the way home, Ashley called and we decided to meet this weekend because Sharon would be in New York with her girlfriends. This was perfect because Ashley could meet my boys this weekend.

I took the boys to Chucky Cheese Pizza early Saturday morning to play. Allen was afraid of Chucky and his friends, especially when the music was played so we sat on the other side where he wouldn't see them. I purchased enough coins to keep them occupied for a couple of hours but before they started playing I wanted Ashley to meet them. She came in and sat at the table next to us. We spoke letting the boys observe this friendly stranger lady sitting beside us. Ashley then came over and squatted by the edge of the table.

She seemed to be having more fun than the boys. Allen didn't take to strangers quickly, but he seemed to be making an exception for Ashley. While they played I ordered pizza. After they wore her out, she brought them back to the table. Almost out of breath, she was carrying Allen and holding onto John's hand. Then she collapsed in the seat. I asked John if he wanted her to have pizza with us. He smiled and hunched his shoulders.

"Ask her, John," I said. John shook his head as if to say no way. She came over and asked John and he said yes. She asked Allen and got no response. After three slices John was ready to play. I commented to Ashley about how good she was with the boys and she went on to say that she was good with their daddy, too. She always had a great sense of humor. Ashley went on to tell me that she felt connected and complete with me. Ashley was very serious about our relationship.

We played with the boys until we ran out of tokens and then we left. The boys enjoyed her. She was already planning for the next event. I took the boys home and we took a nap. Sharon called to check on her babies. It sounded like she was having a great time with all the noise going on in the background. She asked me about five times how the boys were doing. This was a change. I guess it was the apple martinis. Then she finally hung up so that I could get back to sleep. Then my mother called and wanted to come over, but I told her that we were on our way out. I wanted Ashley to keep me company tonight after the boys were asleep.

Ashley called my phone, and I watched it vibrate in my right hand. In my left hand, I held my vodka and cranberry juice. She told me that she was outside. We acted like we were meeting for the first time like teenagers when their parents were away.

I had a surprise for her. It was ecstasy. Neither of us had ever tried it. Tonight was going to be special. My connected manager Clarence gave the pills to me. She came in and gave me a hug. She seemed to be very happy. I motioned with hand signals for her to follow me into the kitchen. She was smiling with excitement. I poured us a glass of water. She whispered, "Water?"

I said, "Yes" and showed her the pills. She asked what they were. I crossed my fingers into the form of an X. She did a silent scream while squeezing me tight. We took them and I went to check on the boys. They were sound asleep. I returned to the kitchen where we talked for a while. She wanted to know all about the X and where it came from.

After about twenty minutes she touched my hands and looked at me with a goofy smile asking me if I felt something. I started kissing her passionately. The X had definitely kicked in. We tore at each other like crazy. It was nonstop. We always had passionate sex but this was beyond us. Every touch was magnificent. Magnified by ten; it felt like our bodies were wax melting into each other. We couldn't get enough. We were reaching climax after climax, each more shattering than the last.

The passion subsided then started all over again until we found ourselves entangled on the sofa making love in the highest form. Then she pulled herself away from me trying to cover her body. I did not know what was going on until I looked up and there he was right in front of us. It was John standing before us watching. Our eyes met briefly. I grabbed my robe and quickly picked him up and whisked him back to bed. Luckily he was sleepwalking. Man that was close. Ashley asked if everything was all right and I told her that he was sleepwalking and he didn't see anything. We decided to end it for the night. But we could have gone all night long. We talked on the phone all night after she left because I knew that she was vulnerable with ecstasy in her system and I didn't want anybody taking advantage of her.

It was Monday afternoon when Sharon came home. After dinner we sat around watching television. I could tell that the boys missed her because they wanted to tell her everything about their weekend. She was eager to hear what went on. Just as I was hoping it would not come up, John told her about Chucky Cheese and that nice lady who played and ate pizza with us. I had to explain it away. Sharon wanted to know who she was. I didn't answer her but just laughed like it was far fetched

She went to bed and I sat in the car and talked on my cell phone. I guess she woke up and noticed that I wasn't there and called my cell phone several times. I didn't answer her calls. So she came into the garage as she dialed my number. I told Ashley that I had company.

Sharon tugged and pulled on the door trying to get to me but the door was locked. She banged on the window then yelled at me and threw the phone against the truck shattering it into many pieces, while asking if I was talking to that bitch from Chucky Cheese. I started the engine, let up the garage door and drove off. She called me all night, but I didn't answer. I spent the night at Ashley's place. Ashley laughed at me when I walked through her door wearing my pajamas. I didn't mind.

Traffic was at a standstill on Interstate 77. I was relaxing as I listened to classical music. I was prepared today to even enjoy a traffic jam. I couldn't wait to get to the terminal because those guys were hilarious. As soon as I walked into the terminal my eyes met Clarence's, and immediately he began to laugh. He asked me what was popping and I said "X". Clarence and I laughed and joked with the drivers before they went on the road. We made our rounds to make sure that everybody was good to go. Once the drivers were on the road, Clarence and I went for our usual breakfast, and I couldn't wait to tell him about my experience with the "X".

A couple hours later it was lunchtime and all the drivers were hanging around discussing the upcoming NBA game between the Charlotte Bobcats and the Los Angeles Lakers. Now that was one game I'd love to see. Clarence said it was a must for me to be at an NBA game. He compared the experience to having Ecstasy without the sex, so he vowed that if I attended he would take care of me. We all met at the terminal before the game where we did drinks and smoked some weed. I had my usual Grey Goose and cranberry. We all were dressed in the thugged out look with the Lex, the Beamers and the Benz. Half of them worked for me. They were driving the luxury cars and had the bling bling.

We arrived at the game and I could tell that they were

ready for anything. Everybody was feeling right and they were about to get *krunk*, as they would say. As we walked into the place, I thought I was with rock stars because everybody was speaking and waving. I thought we would stop at the concession stand, but we went directly to our seats where a concession stand worker was there waiting to take our orders. They waited on us the entire night— happily for the sizeable tips. We still had beer and even more Grey Goose. So this was what VIP felt like. The announcer came over the loud speakers to introduce the players. The excitement built inside of me in a way similar to the ecstasy. I was having the most fun I've had in years.

I had to call Ashley to let her know about the wonderful time I was having. The noise level was so high I could barely hear her, but we managed. She told me that she had a new job as an apartment manager at a new apartment complex. I wanted her to experience the type of fun I was having at an NBA game so I invited her to attend one with me as a celebration of her getting a new job. She agreed.

I called Sharon to see how the boys were doing and they were asleep. She wanted to know if I was coming home for the evening and I wasn't. As soon as I hung up the phone several sexy ladies sat between me and the crew. I didn't know where they came from, but they were put together like models. Clarence knew them and told me that they were down for whatever.

I liked Clarence because he was real. We hung out together all night and the guys didn't bother me anymore about women because they knew that Ashley was on my mind. I guess the frequent phone calls from her gave it away. After the game I think that I had too much to drink. Because I couldn't drive, I spent the night at Clarence's place. The guys gave me a hard time because it took me three days to recover from the night of drinking. My stomach was hurting worse than ever before. I thought that the pain would never stop.

My first day back I worked in the Columbia terminal. It was lunch time when I received a call from Sharon stating that a certified first class letter from the IRS had arrived. I left the office immediately. The letter stated that there was a filing of a federal tax lien and our rights to a hearing. I immediately called Ms. Elizabeth. She said that the money was getting tight and she had been stressing the importance of making cuts without jeopardizing our service obligations, but she had not received a response from Pete. I made a request for us to meet right away with Pete present.

I made several attempts to contact Pete, but he was not answering his phone. I assumed something was wrong. I went to his house. When I arrived I noticed a truck in his driveway that I had never seen before. I repeatedly rang the door bell, but still no answer. Maybe, he had a guest and didn't want to be disturbed. He was very secretive about his significant other and never talked about his love life. We needed to take care of business right now. I returned to the office to meet with Ms. Elizabeth and go over the numbers with a fine tooth comb once again. Our truck payments were still eating up our budget along with

driver accidents, rentals and regular maintenance. To add
to the misery, Pete was supposed to be working on this and
he was nowhere to be found. Ms. Elizabeth went to work
again and created another proposal to present to the IRS.
The proposal was accepted with stipulations. If for any
reason our arrangements were defaulted on, it would be
immediately thrown into lien status.

So after the hearing we implemented the cuts and re-
ductions as stated in the proposal. I took my old route
back to save on payroll. We had to do everything possible
to save the business.

Even though I was driving again, it still didn't save the
company much money. With the increase of gas prices,
driver accidents and preexisting expenses there may have
been a few dollars remaining. And the leftovers were what
Pete and I had to split, which was nothing. After several
months without having an income, things at home were
getting tight. Bill collectors began calling more often and
the utility companies were threatening to disconnect our
services. Sharon was beyond stressed. The entire time I
was worrying about my boys because I didn't want them to
see any drastic changes. If I had any entertainment Ashley
made sure of that, but our relationship was experiencing
difficult times as well.

We were arguing and fighting more often. She would
punch, scratch and bite me if she got close enough. I
would throw her down and pull her hair because I knew
she hated that.

Our most recent fight started when I called her at

work. I thought we were having a great conversation and I understood she was at work, but while we were on the phone someone came into her office, she spoke, erupted into a giddy laugh, and immediately told me that she would call me back later. Before I could respond, she hung up. Instantly I was in a rage because the voice I heard in the background was the voice of a man. I stopped delivering packages and went straight to her job. I stalked into the building. She spoke to me and gave me a friendly smile like everything was great. I stared into her eyes as I got closer.

I could see the anger building in her eyes as she told me that she had someone in the back and walked away. I began to think the worst that she had this dude in the back office while I am standing here. Not for one second did it occur to me that I might have been overreacting. I was angry and hurting that she would do something like this to me... I then walked into the backroom where they were, expecting to see who she found so interesting. There stood this old unattractive maintenance guy repairing the air conditioning unit. He spoke to me and Ashley frowned at me. I felt like an idiot. I said good-bye and she didn't say a word. She thrived on being professional and to have her integrity questioned was the worst thing you could do to her.

I called her cell phone, and she didn't answer. I called her office, and she hung up as soon as she recognized my voice. I knew I had messed up, and it was going to take a great deal to fix it. I had accused her of cheating and had come to her job with an attitude. She was supposed to be angry.

Things were getting hectic. John had to stop his karate class. Sharon was calling asking what we were going to eat because the children were hungry. I needed to do something and fast. My only hope was to ask my mother for more money. I really didn't want to do that. Once again I felt like a failure.

The next morning I arrived to some good news from Pete. He said that the trucks were paid off and he was awaiting a call from Ms. Elizabeth to tell us the difference it would make in our budget. I had already figured that one out. It was more money to pay the IRS.

I then went to my truck to load up for the day. While loading, I came across the same type of large package I thought I've seen before. I remembered delivering this package because it was in a high crime and drug area. There were always a few cars parked there but no one answered the door. I would leave the package on the front door step and circle back around the block then it would be gone. I put the package on my truck but not into the system.

Once I was finished loading I headed out to my route. Instead of starting my route right away, I stopped in a grocery store parking lot near my first stop, looked around to make sure the coast was clear. I opened the box. Its contents were packed, wrapped and sealed tight. When I saw what it was I cut the seal and opened it and a strong smell of cocaine assailed me. I quickly wrapped it back up and rolled down the windows to release the smell. It was uncut pure white powder that was compressed into a big block of chalk. It took my breath away as I gagged from its aroma.

———————————

I rushed to my mother's house to the garage where I kept my boat and jet skies. I hid the package in a safe place where no one could find it. I then rushed back to my route to make service on the rest of the packages. I was nervous and sweating with a thousand thoughts running through my head. I tried to figure out what the hell I was doing. I knew it was crazy, but I couldn't turn back now. We needed the money and this could be the ticket to get my family and me out of the financial crisis, at least temporarily. I finished my deliveries and headed to the liquor store. I needed a drink.

Chapter 9
Strange Relationships

Once I calmed down, I began making some calls. I called an old partner of mine who I knew needed a job. I trusted him because we've done some work in the past and he was no stranger to it. Jay was ready to work and appreciated the opportunity. I then called Clarence and told him that I couldn't talk right then, but it was urgent that he come to the Columbia terminal on the afternoon route from Charlotte.

We meet at the terminal and I didn't go into the details of why and how. I gave Clarence five ounces to see how he moved it. He smelled it and asked how much I wanted back and how soon. We met at lunchtime and he gave me the money and I gave him ten more ounces and told him two weeks.

The terminal was sending us messages inquiring about the missing package. The system showed that this was the last place it was traced. We sent a message back stating that we didn't have it nor had we seen it. That evening while on his last day of training on pick ups Jay and I were at a stop when a car pulled up very close to us. A guy got out while talking on his cell phone as if something was about to go down. He wanted to know if we knew about his package. We told him that we didn't know anything about the package that he was inquiring about. He then got back into his car, and they drove away. I was a little concerned, but I didn't want to overreact. A couple of days later Jay called me and told me that the same guy along with another carload of guys cornered him at a gas station inquiring about that same package. One of the guys was convinced that we took it and was ready to go to war over it. Jay told him that he was a new driver who just started working and one of them believed him. Then they asked about me and why I wasn't with him. Jay told them that I had trained him. I told Clarence what happened and he said that he didn't think they would come after Jay, but we both needed to watch our backs.

While in the back office shortly after I talked with Clarence, I looked out the window and saw those same guys driving into the parking lot. I didn't think someone would make a big fuss over a missing drug package. It could have been a set up. I guess everybody needs money, and they probably had someone thinking that they took it. They asked a few questions about the package and the driver. They wanted to know what time he was coming back into the terminal and said they would wait until his return. Now I hit the panic button. I called Clarence and told him what happened. I would have called some of my people from home, but everybody knows everybody. Clarence assured me that they would be there in two hours.

An hour and forty minutes later he called to meet me. I gave him directions to Jay's route off the exit. They rolled up four cars deep. Clarence was still in uniform as he rode with Jay. Two cars followed Jay and Clarence and the other two followed me back to the terminal. We kept in touch with our two ways. Here I was surrounded by strangers with the passion to survive. This is what these guys lived and died for. I didn't know them personally nor did I know why or how they got to this point to be here with me. I guess we all had a story to tell. We were all connected because of the love of one man, Clarence. Talk about strange relationships. They were here for one reason and one reason only.

When those guys showed up again they were not leaving alive. Where was the love? Better question: what was love? My drivers were coming in. We saw them but they didn't see us. It was like out of sight, out of mind. As we sat there waiting I began to think deeply. I reflected back to the kid in me. I always had the street love. I could count on the rougher people from the area near my father's church almost as soon as I met them. For some reason, they always had my back. Now, I gripped my artillery tight as my heart beat with rage and fear. I lost myself in my pain as I squeezed the loneliness, emptiness, the hurt and rejection I felt. I put all of myself into the anger until the anger became hate. I was hoping they showed because I wanted to release every ounce of it from my body. Maybe those who surround me were feeling the same way. Now thinking of my boys and my family I asked myself, who do you love? I saw their faces, their smiles. I could hear their innocent sweet voices calling out to me. "What are you doing? Daddy, can we play catch? Daddy, I'm glad that we're buddies." It didn't have to be this way. I could feel the tears filling my eyes. I never embraced anger so tightly with the love that I had in my heart. It was thunder and lightning like a tropical storm raging inside of me. What was I thinking? I had put myself and everyone that loved me in jeopardy.

The guys were a no show. Clarence and Jay came to my car as we shook hands with all of his people. I stood face to face with Clarence and he shook my hand and said that if they ever came back or anything else just call and they would be back in full force.

His partners agreed. I knew that they would be there if I needed them. I knew Jay was okay because he never rode alone if you know what I mean. We both had people we could call in case of an emergency.

All I wanted to do was get home to my family. When I returned my boys were asleep, and I was glad because I reeked of stale alcohol. I showered and got into bed. I prayed a silent prayer, speechless now. I thought about everything that had happened to me from my past to the present. Some things words couldn't express. The next day I sent a dozen tulips, one of each color and a card expressing the things words can't say. *I miss you and want to see you.* I went to Ashley's job, where she greeted me with a

WENDELL PRIESTER

warm hello and a beautiful smile. I sat and waited as she attended to her clients. When she finished her meeting, she came over and gave me a huge kiss and a hug. We talked for a moment and I could tell that something was on her mind. My heart dropped. Now what? I asked myself. I couldn't take another crazy moment. I immediately thought her falling for another guy. She paused and took a deep breath and told me about her experience at the strip club. She said that one of the strippers had come over and licked her vagina. She went on to say how ashamed she was. I got up and left without saying a word. She tried to stop me, but I was gone. I don't know what happened to me. My mind just went blank for a moment. She called my cell and I didn't answer. I wish I could have been there when that happened but that was not the reason I was upset. I thought maybe this was what she wanted to do. Could I trust her? If it was a guy then it was over for sure. I felt I had to let her feel isolated for a while. As much as I wanted to console her, she didn't need to think that it was okay or acceptable. I was her protector. She said that she was sorry many times over. She confessed that she stayed in the shower for hours trying to wash away the dirty feelings and she never felt any cleaner. She felt violated. I knew that she was waiting for me to tell her that it wasn't that bad and that it was not the end of the world. So the next phone call I received from her I answered. I wanted to be there for Ashley when and wherever she needed me. I told her that I was not upset with her. She was so relieved to hear that and then asked me to drop by.

When I got to Ashley's place I could hear loud music. I knocked on her door and turned the knob the door came open. I walked inside and saw boxes everywhere with all of her things packed. I headed to the kitchen where the music was coming from. There she stood in front of the refrigerator fixing a drink with her back towards me. I threw my keys on the counter; she turned her head to me like a video vixen. Her lips parted with no words escaping. It was a strange and sexy movement like pain and pleasure. She wore a sexy black wig that graced the length of her shoulders and covered her left eye in secrecy. A white lace thong and beautifully French manicured toes encased in white stilettos completed her ensemble.

She stared deep into my eyes and she walked past me in silence. I asked myself, what the hell? But I loved it. I followed her into the living room and sat on the sofa. She walked over to me and whispered in my ear. "Call me Passion," she said seductively. She began to dance like I've never seen before. This was strange and spontaneous and turning me on, exactly what I wanted. She stood before me with her long statuesque legs straight and tall. Then she began to drop it like it was hot as she shook her tail feather to perfection. She rubbed my legs as I pulled out a roll of hundreds.

From our different experiences and encounters, we connected on a different level. I knew where hers came from but she had no idea about mine. I tipped her with twenties as she smiled at me. She removed the money from her thong and gathered it in her hand. She continued to dance as she slowly removed her thongs and gave me a lap dance. What more could I ask for? I never once had to ask for sex, attention or affection. That's the way I thought it should be. We made sure that we took care of each other's needs. That was a pleasure for us both to be able to do that for each other.

I woke up the next morning lying beside her. I stared at her thinking about last night and what she meant to me. I gently rubbed her body as she awoke and turned towards me. She was still wearing her makeup and wig.

We talked about her packing. She explained that she planned to move back with her mother for six months to save money and have a house built for us. This way she could pursue a career in acting and modeling. I was impressed with her being focused and having a plan. I really needed to figure out how I was going to do this.

Chapter 10
Where is the Love?

The next morning, I walked into the room and Sharon immediately began her condescending tirade. "Sooooo, you decided to come home?" she said in a bitter tone

"Yes, I couldn't find anything else to do," I snapped.

"If you are so unhappy with us then why do you stay?" she asked, calmly.

"I stay because of my boys. They are all that I have and I will never leave them. Why do you stay?" I asked her. "You constantly snap at them and me. I never see you smile. Forget about laughing and having a few jokes; that is totally out of the question. You offer no affection. We haven't had sex in god knows when. You say you don't like the way you look. You don't even look in the mirror. I've tried to make you happy. It is obvious that I can't, or you are not willing to be happy. I'm beginning to think that you only want me here to complain to all the time. I told you that you were making it hard for me. I have nothing to work with here.

"It's not you. I don't know what is wrong with me," she said in a confused tone.

"Get some help," I said. The immediate silence stretched through the rest of the night. We both slept in bed with our backs to each other like strangers.

Sunday morning came and there was still silence between us as we were preparing for church. The phone rang and I got this strange feeling that this call was not going to be a pleasant one. So I rushed to answer it. I'm glad that I did because it was Ashley. I told her that I couldn't talk. Then the phone rang again. I was really tense by now. I was telling myself that this had better not be her calling me back because I would explode.

This time it was Sharon's mom. She had called to tell us that she had decided to retire. I thought a lot of Mom and I told her that was great news. She wanted to talk with Sharon, but Sharon didn't seem to be too happy to talk to her and I didn't ask her why. We went to church and attended Sunday school where we mingled and talked to everyone like nothing was wrong between us. We picked John up from his class after Sunday school and headed to the sanctuary for morning worship. I could imagine the thoughts swirling in Sharon's head trying to make sense of or find the answers to the questions and problems we were having. My mind was flooded as well. I was hoping for inspiration to maybe point me in the right direction.

The music began to play and we stood to sing to open the morning worship. I felt the release of some of the pressure, but my mind was still racing and searching for answers. Then I felt a small hand grab mine. I looked down at John and gave him a smile. Then I noticed that he had placed Sharon's hand in mine. John looked at the both of us; Sharon and I looked at each other, and then looked away. In the middle of our differences we found ourselves seriously considering a divorce. Was this a sign? What did it mean? This definitely put a twist on my thoughts. After church we went to the park, as we always did on Sunday, so the kids could play. Sharon and I talked without making eye contact.

After all of the times, we'd had this conversation; I didn't believe things would change. Still, I was willing to try again for the sake of my family. I worked at the Columbia Terminal that next day. I had a lot of issues on my mind. One of the hardest things I ever had to do was make a decision between my wife and my soul mate based on how much time and influence I wanted to give and share with them. The questions I had to answer were which one was worth more to me or is it about me and would I be of any good to anyone.

It was ten o'clock in the morning and I needed a stiff drink. I called Ashley to arrange for her to meet me at the park and I didn't tell her why. She was dying to know. Meanwhile, I received a call from Ms. Elizabeth and it wasn't good.

She told me that the cancer had rapidly spread throughout her body and that we could not make the IRS payments that we promised. The bills would pile up and soon we could expect our vendors to cut us off. She apologized and told us that we needed to start preparing for the worst.

Maybe this was the day for bad news. I arrived in the parking lot of the park and there was a car following me constantly blowing its horn. I parked next to Ashley's car and the car parked next to me. I waved and recognized that it was a member from my father's church who served on the Youth Group committee with me. She seemed to be happy to see me. She gave me a big hug and began to tell me how proud she was and everybody else was of me for having my own business and a beautiful family. She laughed and joked about me not taking over the church. I was holding on to all of my emotions to keep from breaking down in front of her. If only she knew what I was going through with the business and my beautiful family. Then she looked in Ashley's direction as if she didn't want to know. She immediately said, "Good to see you," and she was gone.

If she was just a minute later she would have seen everything. I never thought about becoming a cheater or committing adultery. I was so caught up in our love relationship that I never thought about it as cheating. My actions went against my beliefs. I never thought I would have a bad marriage, but who knows where life will take us. If we all could make the right choices every time then I would be telling a different story.

Besides, no one cared about how I came into this situation. All they saw was that I was wrong. Once my old church member left, Ashley got out of the car and asked who that lady was. I didn't want to go into that because what I had to tell her was hard enough. "What's up?" she asked. I took a deep breath and told her what happened in church on Sunday with John and Sharon. Ashley then looked away and the tears poured down her face.

"This is so hard for me. I just can't leave them," I said, as the tears streamed down my face. We both were engulfed in tears. The hurt was unbearable. She fell against the baseball field fence and slid to the ground. I tried lifting her limp body from the ground but she pushed me away refusing my help. She came to her feet and slowly walked away as the rain showers began to fall. I called out her name and, as if suddenly filled with a wild energy, she sprinted to her car. She pulled off like a blaze of lightening. I sat in my car, thinking. I felt like there was no use of continuing to write this story. It was true lies for the sake of convenience. After waking from my drunken stupor with the usual sour taste in my mouth and the terrible stomach pains, I drove away quickly. I didn't want to go home.

I needed someone to talk to, and I couldn't talk to Ashley. I wished my father would say something to me. He reminded me of God, or perhaps God reminded me of my father. I knew that He loved me, but He just wouldn't talk to me. Help me to see it clearly. Where was I missing it? Is this love? I went to my mother's house and rung the doorbell. All the lights in and outside of the house came on and she opened the door and I walked in. She frowned as the alcohol aroma wafted from me.

I told her that I was losing the business; I couldn't find Pete, Sharon and I were trying but things were not working out. I was in love with another woman. And on top of that I couldn't stop drinking and everything kept spinning around and around. Mama began to stare off into space, speechless. I saw the pain in her eyes like it had been there for many years. She spoke out saying that Sharon loved me and the children needed their father and that I needed to let the woman go.

"I already have," I said.

"Good," she said.

Sharon's mother kicked off her retirement by treating us to a vacation. We already planned to take the boys to Disney World. Her being there with us improved our relationship, especially with the boys. Sharon seemed to enjoy catching up lost time with her as well. She wanted to know if I was going to lose the business and how was I going to afford it if Mama didn't pay. I had money put away, but I didn't tell her about it. I knew we had to start over so I was planning to sell my BMW and the house to downsize to something more economical. We needed to establish a college fund for the boys. I wanted my children to have a head start on their future. Most parents have failed in that department and I didn't want to be one of them.

We vacationed in a nice three bedroom home near Disney where we had easy access and convenience. It was John and Allen's first time there, so they entered the gates it was like it was heaven. They were so excited. We were on the go for at least eight hours straight nonstop. We stopped approximately twenty minutes to eat. The evenings belonged to me. I enjoyed the different atmosphere and scenery from the same day to day hustle and bustle of work back at home. I wanted to relax with my family. For some strange reason I wasn't resting well. I had this uneasy feeling in my stomach that made me nauseated and interrupted my sleep. I had a feeling that my drinking was either causing it or making it worse

We had a chance to see all of the Disney characters from the boy's favorite television shows. I was nominated and won Daddy of the Year. I just didn't know about next year's vacation. This one was hard to top.

It was definitely the stuff of lifelong memories. We must have ridden every ride in the park twice. And each line we stood in to get on the ride we waited from thirty minutes to an hour. Even with all the fun I was having with my family, I still couldn't get Ashley off my mind. I would call her cell phone and hang up before she'd answer. It was not easy for me to let go. We all were having a great time but Sharon and I were not connecting as we thought we would. If it didn't have anything to do with the children, then Sharon and I were in our own worlds. I could see that her mother recognized that but didn't say anything about it. At the end of our week vacation, John was ready for our plane ride, but Allen wasn't so sure about the taking off or the landing part.

After our vacation my mother- in- law, Gracie, and I felt like we were getting to know each other a little better.

I thought she was pretty cool, so we decided to go out and have a few drinks. I think Sharon would have been different if she had been raised by her. She asked many questions even though she was my mother in law. I didn't mind. She knew something was weighing heavy on my mind, so I told her about the business. She told me that there would be other opportunities if things didn't go well and I really appreciated her words of encouragement. They lifted my spirits.

On our way back to the house she told me that she learned a lot about me, more than I knew. I laughed but she was serious. I thanked her for sharing the evening and her insight.

My life seemed to be becoming a little more stable, at least for the moment. This particular recovery meeting I arrived early seeking more inspiration. I talked to others who also arrived early, and they seemed to be coping well. Before we separated ourselves into small groups we came together for devotion. There were many there from many different walks of life, struggles and habits, but they all were there for the same thing...help. The appearance of some was obvious, but for others you would think that they had everything under control. When we separated into groups, there was more one on one contact where we came up close and personal with the affects of addiction on our families, friends and coworkers. Most of us had relapsed because either we got caught up in the moment of anxiety when we are tense, angry, hurting, exhausted or resentful. During that moment you try to relax and think clearly. That's the idea, but it does not happen that way all the time. God knows that I needed to be here because our study chapter focused on Forgiveness. I took a deep breath because this very word rang so loudly in my ears I knew it was just for me. It forced me to examine my relationship with my father.

I realized that I had to let go of the past. I was hurting myself and others around me by holding onto it. If I expected God to forgive me, I had to forgive others. As we progressed into the chapter, I realized that my unforgiving heart kept me going back to my addiction. My father wasn't physically present for me to ask him those unanswered questions, but I released all that I held against him. Once I spoke the words of forgiveness, I felt a sense of relief like that of a freed prisoner. My only wish was for him to be here to receive my forgiveness though he may have had a problem with showing his love and affection. Still, I wanted to display my love and understanding so bad. It was like a light had come on and I saw not him but me. I could see what I could have done and the other direction I should have taken. There was one person present at this moment that was necessary for me to forgive and that was me. The guilt, the shame and all the dirt and selfishness— I needed to release. I forgave myself and others. The next step was to obtain the ultimate forgiveness and that was from God.

Would this be the end of all of my problems? No, it was only the beginning. It was the freedom from resentment and bondage. Something I was carrying and didn't need to. I didn't know if or when I would drink again and I wasn't worried about it. I wasn't going to stop pushing towards recovery because for once I could see that this was sufficient for me. In God's own perfect timing He would talk to me but He wasn't obligated to me or anyone else. I wasn't going to doubt who He was or our relationship.

I drove home from that meeting with a clear mind. Something I'd never truly left with before. I got home, took a shower and got into bed. I said a prayer and laid there in the dark. My mind was clear enough to allow me to fall into a peaceful sleep. I dreamed of fields of green with trees and wild flowers dancing in the innocent noon day haze. I saw a child running in the distance. My palms sweated in anticipation as to who and why he ran as if his life depended on his breaking free. The closer he came I could see the texture of his sandy reddish hair in the sunlight. His face was riddled with concern and confusion. I pulled up my blue coveralls in the crotch with my left hand as I bent down on one knee. I reached out to him with open arms to save him from whatever chased him to me. I wanted to let him know that he was okay because he was here with me. As he came into view I noticed that he was not my son and I was not his father. He was my father running to his father saying, "I'm sorry, I wasn't a man. I'm going to be a man. Please don't beat me, I'll stop crying." Whatever caused him to say these things I didn't know why but he agreed that he would do it. Only he and his father knew why. He asked for forgiveness from his father but couldn't overcome whatever happened between them. Maybe he wanted to be free of it and could not talk about it with me or anybody else. What he gave me was possibly all that he had to give. I woke up in a cold sweat breathing heavy.

Sharon asked if I was okay. I immediately went into my boys' room and stared at them in the dim lamp light. Their faces were so peaceful. I wanted to tell them right then and there that I loved them with all of my heart. I wanted to wake them from their sleep and hold them so close to me so that they could feel the love from my soul. I wanted to give them all of me every waking minute of the day even while they slept. Had I ever been this precious to my own father? What did all this mean? What was I going to do now to make a difference in my life? I didn't know, but I had put a lot behind me to move forward without resentment in my heart.

And still I was thinking of Ashley every moment of the day. I wondered where she had gone, what she was doing and if she was okay. I wanted to know if she was missing me the way that I was missing her. I wondered if she had found another lover. She didn't deserve the pain that I brought. I still would call her number and hang up before it rang. I eventually called her using * 67 to block the caller ID and she answered in frustration but I didn't say anything and she hung up.

I called a second time and she answered again and once again I didn't say a word. I had so much to say to her. I wanted to tell her how much I loved and missed her. All

I could do was hold the phone breathing real hard with anxiety, listening to her soft sweet voice say, "If you are not going to say anything I am going to hang up." I couldn't. As much as I wanted to, I could not speak because old wounds would reopen.

The next day I pulled into the Columbia terminal and there were new trucks aligned in sequential order like when we first received them. This looked familiar. The only difference is that it was the beginning of the end.

As I walked to my office our employees were asking questions as if they didn't know what was going on. Not given any information, the drivers went through their normal routines of getting through their routes on time.

The Contracts Manager called me into his office. On my way there I met Chuck on the way and he passed me with a peculiar look on his face like a cat that caught the canary but he didn't say a word. I thought that was odd. When I got into his office the contract manager handed me several faxes from Elizabeth dated a month ago with all of our financial information including the IRS statement containing information about levying and liens on our accounts. There were also documents that listed our company budgets. That explained why the new trucks were parked.

He told me that one of his managers found the documents near the fax machine. I thought back to the many times I told Elizabeth not to fax our information unless she knew that either myself or Pete would be on the receiving end but that was irrelevant now. I couldn't do anything about it.

I took a deep breath and exhaled because I knew what he was about to say to me wasn't good. "I'm sorry it didn't work out. I don't know how you guys survived on this budget," he said.

"Where is Pete?" he asked. I told him that I didn't know. After my conference call with the managers to tell them the status of the company and to inform their drivers to park all vehicles outside, I headed over to Pete's house to tell him the news.

When I arrived at his house, I saw the same truck in his driveway parked next to his car. I rang his doorbell twice and he didn't respond. I was beginning to wonder about this guy so I walked around his house looking in every window to see if he was all right.

To my surprise when I came upon his bedroom window I saw him lying across the bed in a man's arms. I couldn't believe my eyes. I never thought that he was gay. I was at a loss for words. I wasn't angry. I just wanted to know why he didn't tell me. I thought we were closer than that. Even though I didn't agree with it, he was still my long time friend and partner. Well, it was not like he knew about my relationships. I guess some things we tend to keep to ourselves.

I sat in the car thinking about what I needed to do. I had to shut down the company as soon as possible. I thought about the progress Sharon and I had made and I know that this would be a setback. I drove all the way home trying to find the right words to tell Sharon. I got home and the boys were as happy as ever. They greeted me at the door with huge hugs as they jumped into my arms screaming, "Daddy! Daddy!" I walked in and spoke to Sharon and her mother. They saw the emotional drain on my face I asked if Sharon wanted to join me for dinner. I thought that this was a nice gesture for us to salvage and build upon what we had left in our marriage. She accepted. As we were getting dressed we exchanged pleasantries and complimented each other on how we looked for the evening. We kissed the boys good night and I gave them their usual tickling to make them laugh. Sharon and I headed to the downtown area to dine at the Motor Supply Co. On our way there we listened to Frankie Beverly and Maze play softly in the background. She didn't have much to say.

I couldn't take her usual negative conversations of criticizing others and complaining. Although at this moment, I couldn't blame her. She was bored and frustrated with being a stay-at-home mom. She wanted to work and interact with others. And I encouraged her to do so. We continued the conversation about her working when we were seated. I could tell that it grabbed her interest. I supported the change for her sanity but my motives were to get her support on helping me as well. I still wanted that sense of togetherness. We ordered a bottle of Riesling wine, and I casually presented the news of closing down the business. I also told her the plans to keep us going as a family which I thought could have been worst.

After my telling her the news I told her that this would be a great time for her to begin work and interact. She grew silent and stoic. When I asked her what she thought about the plans, she replied by saying that now she knew why I wanted to have this spontaneous dinner. It was only for the purpose of delivering bad news. I tried to be encouraging by telling her that we still had a lot to be thankful for. We would make the best of it.

I held my glass to toast, but she didn't. She barely spoke a word for the rest of the evening. I had more conversation with the waitress than I had with her. I looked directly into her eyes as she day dreamed. I don't know where her mind went. I received a phone call. It displayed as unknown on my cell phone screen. "Hello," I said and paused. "Hello," there was no response. I thought could it be Ashley, which brought a smile to my face. I took a gulp of my wine and I laughed softly to myself. "If you are there, press the pound key once," I whispered. She did.

"If you miss me press twice." She pressed it continuously. I laughed.

Nowhere in sight and without any words had Ashley brought laughter and happiness to me. She accompanied me that evening for a romantic candlelight dinner with soft classical jazz, tingling wine glasses and festive voices in conversation. I wouldn't have minded dancing and celebrating the good news of being out of business. What was most important was the opportunity for us to be together and indulge in each other. Sharon asked who I was talking to. I was back to reality. I had to cut my romantic evening short and return to solitary confinement. I motioned my head to her to say no one. I told Ashley that I was in a meeting and I was being rude by being on the phone so I told her good bye.

Our waitress returned to ask us if everything was all right. I suggested that she bring the check. We drove home in silence. I could only imagine what Sharon was thinking. I know what I was thinking. I was thinking of the lovely time Ashley and I shared this evening. It was everything I needed. Sharon's mother wanted to know why we were home so soon. I didn't respond and went to bed immediately.

The next day Gracie hugged me and said that things would work out. I appreciated those words of encouragement, but I wasn't the one who needed them the most. Gracie continued helping us connect as lovers but I think that we both were running out of hope. We were drifting further apart and were ready to accept the way that it was.

Gracie had Sharon and me write down the things we thought were romantic and turned us on. She also wanted us to include an evening we would enjoy the most. Nothing lavish but the kind you can create yourself. It was something she suggested we do on our seventh anniversary. I had to admit that it sounded interesting. I thought it might be fun and be helpful to our relationship. Sharon began working on her list immediately.

Her mother gave me suggestions. Afterwards, I went out to purchase the items that Sharon had on her list. Gracie came along. I thought that Sharon might have some problems with the list I provided. I thought maybe she would have some questions on how I knew so much about lingerie. She rattled off, "What do you like? Sexy baby dolls, dream teams of silk, satin in summer shades, sheer mesh and lace signature sleep wear with stiletto sandals?"

Some men like to be surprised. I love to give surprises. The first and only time I gave Sharon a lingerie surprise turned out to be a disaster. I bought it a size too small and it sent her into depression over her weight.

That was the last time for spontaneous surprises. I tried the surprise thing again. Only this time it was for Ashley. She liked it, gave me a kiss and tried it on for me. I sat there as she modeled sexy lingerie in front of me. She looked like a model straight out of Elle magazine. She got several selections. Maybe that was her plan. If it was then it was well worth it.

I was beginning to compare Ashley and Sharon and that was something I didn't want to do. It was obvious. There was no comparison. At this point I was exploring all options to kick off our seventh anniversary. Sharon got her hair done, a pedicure and a full body massage. I picked her up and took her to an early dinner so that we could enjoy as much as possible. We took a short ride through the countryside of Camden, South Carolina to get to the historical restaurant called Camden South; it was located in an antebellum mansion.

After dinner we walked out into the gathering dusk, holding hands. As we approached the end of the curbside, a horse and carriage pulled up in front of us. The horseman helped us aboard. Sharon looked into my eyes and smiled. I felt a heavy feeling come over my chest. The pressures from my emotions and feelings and the struggles we had in the past—and now this hope—I felt like crying. Maybe this was the connection we needed. I must admit that I was nervous. The gentleman took us on a tour of this small historical city that we both enjoyed. We rode home with the sunroof back listening to Norah Jones. The pale moonlight was exciting and sensual. I felt the night air caress my skin and hug my senses like a new love. I felt a spark of rejuvenation. We returned home and the boys were already asleep. Sharon's mother was dying to know how the evening went. Sharon immediately answered and said that it was nice and she was impressed.

We went to our bedroom. I showered and put on my silk pajama bottoms without the top just as she wanted. She showered and put on what I thought to be my sexy romantic request. I put on some soft jazz and had a chilled bottle of champagne waiting. I was impatiently waiting to see how close she was to my imagination. The doors to the bathroom opened and she walked out. The first thing she saw was the champagne.

"Why do you have that?" she asked

"What?"

"Alcohol, you don't need that."

I shook my head and let out a sigh of disgust. "You have got to be kidding me," I said. "Cotton pajamas and flat furry shoes is that what you are wearing?" I said. Then the phone rang. It was her grandmother.

"Congratulations honey! How is it going?" she asked

"Okay," Sharon said and began a conversation. I got up, changed clothes and told her that I'd be back. Her gaze was blank and empty. I took the bottle of champagne, left the room, and as I passed through the den where Gracie was sitting, she asked, "What's wrong?"

I just shook my head and kept walking. Her mother then joined Sharon. "What happened?" she asked.

"He wanted to drink," she replied.

"This is only one evening to celebrate," Gracie said.

"He didn't like what I was wearing."

"Why did you wear that?" her mother asked.

"This is me."

"I know, baby. It's supposed to be your night together. That is what it's all about."

I got into my car and headed down the street. I turned up the bottle and guzzled several times as I sped away. I drove a block and stopped the car. In anger, I punched the steering wheel and began to cry. There was nothing else between us. I resumed driving thinking that I needed more to drink. The more I drank the more I wanted to talk with Ashley but only got her voice mail. Where could she be?

I ended up sitting in front of Ashley's place still wondering what happened between me and Sharon. I tried answering all the questions that were running through my mind. Were we both too stubborn to make a change for each other? If we changed, who would we become? How much change was too much? Was I who she really wanted? Was she who I really wanted? What had

I done? Had I made a huge mistake by marrying her? Was I making an even bigger one by leaving what I had begun? To complicate it all, I had let the love of my life get away. And, I couldn't drink anymore because I was becoming terribly ill.

I began to vomit blood everywhere. I wanted to get out of the car but I was too weak. I couldn't stop the vomiting. I lay back in the seat to catch my breath then Ashley pulled up beside me wearing a warm smile. As she got closer to my car she saw my condition and she quickly opened the car door. There was blood everywhere.

"Oh my God, Phillip," she cried in horror.

"I have been trying to call you, but you didn't answer."

"I was at the movies with my nieces and nephews. When I got to my car I called you back, but your phone went straight to voice mail." Then she opened my phone and it was dead.

"Open my trunk and get the towel from my golf bag."

She tried to clean me up and help me over to the passenger seat to take me to the Emergency Room. On the way there I vomited more blood twice more. She constantly rubbed my hand while encouraging me to hang on and stop drinking. "We can do it! We all can do it," she murmured, as she took my hand and rubbed it across her stomach. Ashley arrives at the Emergency Room with Phillip. She immediately runs inside to get help while explaining what happened. The doctor and nurses then rush out to the car with a gurney and wheel Phillip through the glass sliding doors. Ashley quickly parks the car and heads back inside .Once they take Phillip into the back room to stabilize him, Ashley hangs around until one of her friends arrives to take her home. The hospital then makes contact with Sharon. She looks at the clock in hopes that the phone call is from Phillip.

"Hello," Sharon says.

"This is the Emergency Room staff at East Brook calling on behalf of Phillip Henry. Is this the Henry residence?"

"Yes, it is."

"May I ask your relation to Phillip Henry?"

"I am his wife."

"Okay, Mrs. Henry, Phillip has lost an enormous amount of blood. He is unconscious but stable in ICU and we are going to keep him until further notice." Kiss my lips, caress my hands and press your body against mine just one more time. I wanted Ashley to do that to me.

After seeing Dr. Paul, Sharon, her mother and the boys were there to take me home. I rode with Sharon while the boys rode with her mother. She didn't mention anything about the last episode; she simply took care of me by gently placing me in the car and driving slowly. We listened to the soft melodies of the piano and the flute play. How soothing. I wanted that peaceful joy to play in my heart forever. I wanted my soul to rest for a little while longer. I felt every note dance down the spine of my back and into the corners of my stomach. I wanted it to be whole again. The moment was so magical. She placed her hands and her heart in mine and mine in hers and we were as one. She kissed me internally and our souls became love. I saw the daffodils and the cherry blossoms when the May flowers bloom.

I felt the earth move and she was mine. I promised to cherish and love her in good times and bad, in sickness and in health until death do us part. She was there for me. My mother arrived and couldn't keep her hands off of me. She rubbed every inch of my body as if to soothe the pain away. Sharon's mom comforted my mom while the boys made my legs into a race track for their toy cars. I lay on the sofa while Sharon made sure we all had everything that we needed. She was the perfect wife.

Knock! Knock! "Hello, Dr. Howard. Another board member told me that the meeting has been delayed by an hour."

I was deep in thought while listening to Phillip's story on tape. Not only did I get to see who he was, I also saw who I was and what I was harboring inside. There was anger, shame, resentment and fear. I realized that I had been holding anger against my father for thirty-six years, for his abandonment when we needed him the most. The shame I felt for not having a father growing up and explaining why another man raised me and helped my mother. The shame of answering the questions of why he left thinking the whole time there was something wrong with me and Mother. Resenting my mother for lifting me over the bridge wall and threatening to end my life before it fully began.

I became almost fearful about sharing my love, affections and feelings, for anyone even my children. From the time I was in my mother's womb I felt unwanted. Against the negatives I'd strived and pushed to become successful externally. Internally, I lay wounded .Thanks to Phillip sharing his story with me, he had made me to take a long hard look within myself and take an honest inventory and have the courage to face change. I saw myself in a different light now.

I gave the committee my word that I would give this project the best attention to make this memorial a success. As I rushed out to my car, I pondered on the changes that were needed and to whom I needed to ask for forgiveness. I started the car and sped off to my mother's house. It's been a long time coming. I arrived and dashed out of the car. I slammed the car door and rang the door bell repeatedly until she opened the door. When she saw me she sensed problems. But I told her what was right.

"I love you, Mom," I said.

"I love you too," she said as she continued to wipe down the counters and do other chores.

"Do you want something to eat?" she asked.

I stopped her from working and grabbed her hands, turned her to face me. I looked deep into her eyes and I told her once again, "I love you and I am sorry for all those years I have been holding onto bitterness towards you. Thank God I can see and share my heart, affections towards you, my father, Cathy and the children. I feel free." I kissed her and gave her a huge hug and told her that I loved her again and that I needed to get to Cathy and the kids and share the good news about my new insights.

As I rushed out of the house my coat got caught on the door handle and it pulled me back, ripping it. I fell down the stairs. Mother asked me if I was okay. I didn't have time to answer at that moment. I sprung back up and continued to run. Then I called out that I was okay. My mother quietly laughed and waved good bye as I sped off from 0 to 60 in 4 seconds. I was never so anxious to see Cathy and the kids.

I wasn't doing too well. I took on a high fever of 105 degrees and I was still having abdominal pain caused by infection. The vomiting of blood was continuous until Sharon called the Emergency Room to send paramedics and they notified Dr. Paul. As I pulled up to the house my family was packed and backing out of the driveway. I jumped out of my car and stopped them by knocking on the window several times. Cathy sat in the front seat, crying. She hesitated in letting the window down. I began apologizing. I told her how sorry I was and that I was terribly wrong. I wanted her to know that I needed her and the children and that I loved them. I told her that I had come to realize what was wrong with me and I needed them to forgive me.

As I knelt down next to the car, my phone rang. It was the hospital. They said that Phillip was on his way back to the hospital. He had a relapse and was losing lots of blood. I asked Cathy to move over because I needed to rush to the hospital. "I'll explain everything on the way," I said. The ambulance arrived quickly. They backed in as Sharon rushed to open the garage door. I hugged my boys tightly

and gave them a kiss. I let them know that I loved them.
They were both afraid and curious. "Why are they taking
Daddy away on that bed with wheels?"

"Is Daddy coming back?"

My mother walked alongside me rubbing and caress-
ing my hands as we got to the doorway. . I saw pain in her
eyes, but she pressed a smile on her lips for my benefit.

They picked me up and carried me down the steps. I
could feel the storm like pulses raging in my gut. Sharon
laid her hands in mine as tears rolled down her face. I
wanted to let her know that everything would be all right.
I told her that I was sorry and she shook her head.

I saw my boys waving to me as they rolled me into
the ambulance. My mother pulled them away from the
window. Sharon and her mother followed the ambulance
to the hospital. As we exited the freeway near the hospital
I felt us taking only left turns. I heard the driver asking
dispatch what was going on up ahead. There were uni-
formed policemen and plain clothes undercovers blocking
the road. The dispatcher replied and said that there was a
drug raid that had a lot of gun activity involved. I knew we
were near my father's church. I hoped that everyone was
okay. Then the driver said that he anticipated respond-
ing to that call. We had to keep taking left turns until we
went full circle. I was driving as fast as I could to get to
the hospital and at the same time explaining to Cathy my
life changing experience and how I saw myself. I wanted
her to know why I hadn't been able to fully express my
love, why I hadn't been who I had promised to be on our

wedding day. I wanted to let her know that I was sorry for all the lost time we spent apart. And now we were rushing to the hospital to meet the very person who was responsible for that change in me.

Chapter 11
A Lesson Before Dying

Here I was in a hospital bed once again attached to more tubes and machines. This time I was conscious and able to feel all the pain, all of which did not come from cirrhosis of the liver but from my heart.

It was for all the people who I loved and those whom I may or may not have had a relationship with. As I noticed the urgency of the nurses and their panic stricken faces, I thought that I wasn't going to make it. I was more afraid for my loved ones than myself. I was nervous and thinking about my boys and how they needed their daddy with them to protect and guide them in the right direction. There was no one else who could love them the way that I could. If I should leave them now, it would be devastating.

Kissing their faces, playing chase, running, laughing and singing made up songs and answering all of their questions even when they didn't make sense... this could not be the end. I had to stop overreacting because it wouldn't make any sense for me to die now. What would my mother do? This would surely tear her apart. Ashley did not even know that I was in the hospital. . My wish at that moment was to be able to tell her how very much I loved her.

The hardest thing I ever had to do in my life was to let her be free. The truth was that I had invited her into a life that Sharon and I built. Having two boys that I adore wouldn't be the same if I left. Even with liberal visitation rights and equal arrangements, nothing could take the place of a dad in the home. But it still remained to be seen if I could give up the love that bound Ashley and me together. At this point only God knew. He was the only one who could help me make it right. Mother said that sometimes dying is the only way out.

We finally made it to the hospital parking garage. I told Cathy the entire story as to how I got to this point in my life. We all raced through the hospital corridors attracting much attention. I knew that we did not have a moment to spare. As we passed the nurse's station they all followed us because they had never seen me with so much emotion. I was crying and running through the hospital with my family. I knew that time was critical. Everyone definitely saw a change in me.

Sharon stood by my bedside crying. As much as we fought and didn't get along, I wanted a chance to try again. Maybe this time I could reach her. You don't miss a good thing until it is gone and I wanted to finish what we started. I realized this time she needed me as her savior. My body felt numb. I had no strength left to say good bye.

My alcohol wracked body started to hemorrhage. All I

heard was Sharon screaming. I began to say, "I don't want to die, God, I am sorry." Far from my purpose, my life was a waste. It had never reached its potential. . Nothing was accomplished. But God was more than able to love me as I was and to lift me up. There was no greater love. Dr. Paul rushed into the room. I could see the tears in his eyes. He had with him his beautiful family but I couldn't hold out any longer. With all that I had left in me I opened my hand.

We held hands and he closed his eyes. I lay across his legs and cried like a baby. I just lost my best friend and I didn't get a chance to thank him. Cathy hugged me from behind along with the children. The room and the hallways were full with staff and friends; their eyes were filled with tears. Phillip thought that he didn't have any accomplishments. But not so…

Phillip's Memorial Park

Phillip put his trust in me. I was a total stranger and he put his life in my hands. Shortly after his passing, I met with his family and explained the entire story within the story. Phillip's book Who Do You Love remained on the Best Sellers list at number five for a record 52 weeks. A movie deal was being negotiated. I had a small hand in its completion.

"Good afternoon everybody, I want to thank you all for coming to celebrate this wonderful historic day. We have gathered here today to celebrate, honor and dedicate this park in the memory of a person who represents the true essence of what this park stands for in our community.

"I am Dr. Paul Howard, President of the Board of Neighborhood Associations. I would like to thank our board members and City Council members who worked so diligently to make this day a reality. This park represents a place of recreation and rest where we can all come together as one to enjoy fellowship with others and with nature. It is a place for families, children, lovers and friends. It is a place for hobbies, games and sports. It is also the pillar of our communities where we nurture, teach and discover talent and new ideas that change our outlook on life.

This is what our honoree represents - new relationships, different outlooks and new beginnings. This park is like a cutting edge medication. It treats, cures, prevents, relieves, improves and preserves. It heals. To understand someone is to see their point of view. To share and show love is like taking your medicine to endure until the end. I took a dose of medicine from a close friend and patient of mine. He brought me to the light to see the big picture beyond myself. We all have thoughts and opinions. He helped me see into myself. His medicine was a long time coming. His struggle was how to make others and himself happy the right way. He died trying to do just that. All of his life he felt that he never accomplished anything but that has changed. I hope that you all get a chance to read his book. If you haven't, I suggest that you do because it has been a life changing experience for me. That is why I stand before you, because he is responsible for that change in me.

"I hope that this park will spark a change in you and make a difference in your lives. My wife Cathy and I were able to rediscover the love and passion we've lost which was there all the time. Now, we are able to take each other's medicine and understand how to make each other happy and content in our relationship. If we took care of each other without selfish agendas then we all would be taken care of. I thank you for the best seller and for all that you have given. Ladies and Gentlemen, I present to you Phillip Memorial Park."

The band played in a muted soft tone. People danced as the festivities began. The children played in the distance as you could hear echoes of laughter and merriment. All of our children played together.

Chapter 12
Finally.....................

It was about time for the Howards to join us. We were going on vacation together. While waiting for them to come, I walked out on the back deck to observe the beautiful sunshine, the sounds of nature, and to listen to the water splashing against the boat as the breeze caressed my face.

I was just enjoying the new change and getting used to a peaceful life. It was about time. At this time in my life, I am thankful for everyday and for every day I am grateful.

"Hi, Phillip."

"Hello, Cathy, Welcome aboard!"

"Hey, Sara and David give me a big hug and kiss. I love you. They are all waiting inside for you."

"Paul, how is it going?"

"Great! Thanks to you. How are you?"

"I couldn't be better. You saved my life."

"So, what are your thoughts about the ending?"

"Absolutely wonderful! I mean, very well written and heartwarming."

"Good! I'm glad that you like it."

Then the captain looked back at us to see if we were ready to cast off. We raised our glasses to toast the success of <u>Who Do You Love</u>? We sailed towards the setting sun; the boat's wake foamed white behind us pointing to the yacht's name on the transom. ***Finally***....

2 Corinthians 5: 17-19

17 Therefore, if anyone is in Christ, he is a new creation; the old has gone, the new has come! **18** All this is from God, who reconciled us to himself through Christ and gave us the ministry of reconciliation: **19** that God was reconciling the world to himself in Christ, not counting men's sins against them. And he has committed to us the message of reconciliation.

CPSIA information can be obtained at www.ICGtesting.com
Printed in the USA
LVOW131608200313

325240LV00002B/213/P